Carl Weber's Kingpins:

The Bronx

Carl Weber's Kingpins:

The Bronx

Marcus Weber

www.urbanbooks.net

Urban Books, LLC
300 Farmingdale Road, N.Y.-Route 109
Farmingdale, NY 11735

Carl Weber's Kingpins: The Bronx
Copyright © 2018 Marcus Weber

ISBN 13: 978-1-945855-56-6
ISBN 10: 1-945855-56-8

First Trade Paperback Printing November 2018
Printed in the United States of America

10 9 8 7 6 5 4 3 2 1

Distributed by Kensington Publishing Corp.
Submit Orders to:
Customer Service
400 Hahn Road
Westminster, MD 21157-4627
Phone: 1-800-733-3000
Fax: 1-800-659-2436

Carl Weber's Kingpins:

The Bronx

by

Marcus Weber

Prologue

"Are you ready?"

Paige looked up, startled. She blinked a few times and looked to her right and smiled. "I guess so," she replied, jamming her right fist into her hip, with her arm bent at the elbow to make an opening for her brother to slide his arm through.

"You look amazing, sis."

Paige's stomach clenched. Her father had said almost those exact words the first time she'd gotten married. *You look amazing, baby girl.*

A small explosion of heat lit in Paige's chest—one part anger, one part sadness—as she thought about her father's nerve when he refused to give her away a second time. She closed her eyes and exhaled. She shook her head, wishing away her worries. She couldn't focus on the past right now. If she did, she might not make it down the aisle this time. And this time, the marriage was a necessity, not just a want.

"You clean up nicely yourself." Paige looked up at her brother, her fake smile perfected now.

It was true. Gladstone Tillary, Jr., had come a long way since his latest stint in rehab. Even with his neck tattoos peeking from his shirt collar, he presented well—classy and sharp. Paige was sorry she'd ever gotten him involved in everything that had happened. Her heart broke every time she thought about how she had turned her back on him in his darkest hour, yet he had stood by her in hers.

"I really appreciate you getting rid of those awful dreadlocks, too," she said, her tone playful.

"Well, they're gone but not forgotten," her brother joked, running his hand over his neatly trimmed hair.

They laughed.

Paige needed the laugh. She'd take anything to ease some of the muscle-twisting tension that had her entire body in knots.

Finally, the low hum of her wedding song, *You* by Kenny Latimore, filtered through the outdoor speakers.

"That's our cue."

Her brother squared his shoulders and tightened his lock on Paige's arm, forcing her closer to him.

"Thank you for being here, Junior," Paige whispered. She meant it. She knew he'd probably endured a harsh berating from their parents for agreeing to give her away. That was the one quality she had always admired most about her baby brother since they were kids. He never cared what her parents said or thought, unlike Paige, who had spent her entire life walking the fine line of being an individual and making her parents happy. She always wanted to be the "good one," as her mother called her.

"C'mon. You know I wouldn't miss the free food and wine," her brother joked.

Paige giggled. Then she got serious. "No wine for you," she chastised in a playfully gruff voice.

"All right. Here we go."

Paige looked down and smoothed her left hand over the fine, hand-sewn iridescent beads on the front of her haute couture gown. She found a lone bead to pick at with the hopes it would help calm her nerves.

"Loosen up. You're a pro at this, right? Second time's the charm?"

Paige parted a quivery-lipped smile. "The way I'm shaking you'd think this was my first time."

She sucked in her breath as she finally stood at the end of the beautifully decorated aisle in the pastoral Breaux Vineyard. One-hundred-year-old weeping willows swayed in the wake of the breeze with their wispy, white bud covered tendrils calling her forward. Pink rose petals dotted the path in the center aisle, and tall silver stanchions holding white and lilac hydrangea globes flanked every other row of white Chiavari chairs. Dreamy, romantic, and heavenly were all words that came to mind.

With her arm hooked through her brother's, Paige plastered on her famous, toothy smile and carefully navigated the vineyard's emerald green lawn in her heels. Collective awestruck gasps rose and fell amongst the guests seated on either side of the decorated bridal path. The absence of her parents and her best friend, Michaela, didn't go unnoticed. But, it was the Cartwrights—Emil, Hayden, and Jackson—who caused Paige to stumble a bit.

Focus, Paige. Focus. She knew they were there to make sure she went through with it, their presence like a threat whispered in her ear. *It'll all be over soon*, she told herself.

Antonio stepped into the aisle to meet her. He wore a smile that said, "I'm trying to make this seem real too." Unlike Paige's penchant for the grandiose, Antonio was simple. He wore a plain black suit, forgoing the obligatory tuxedo, white cummerbund, and shiny shoes.

Paige felt something flutter inside her like a million butterflies trapped in a jar. With everything they'd been through, Paige had lost sight of how handsome Antonio was. He looked more gorgeous now than he had years ago when they were just two young, high school lovebirds. Back then, Antonio was a gangly six-foot-three-inch kid with a bulging Adam's apple and a hairless baby face. Now, he'd transformed into a distinguished gentleman with a neatly trimmed goatee, thick square shoulders that filled out his suit jacket, and a muscular barrel chest. He looked more like a Calvin Klein underwear model than a former professional basketball player. Paige had certainly forgotten. Anger, hurt, bitterness, and the threat of a life sentence had a way of changing perspective, she'd learned.

Antonio took her brother's place at Paige's side. She looked over at him, her heart dancing in her chest.

"Shall we begin with a prayer?" the officiant said, his Bible splayed over his palms.

Paige lowered her eyes.

The day Paige met Antonio, she and her best friend Michaela had snuck out of Michaela's house, thanks to Michaela's mother's love for cheap vodka and loud jazz music. Paige and Michaela had dressed in outfits that they thought made them look older—tight knee-length leather skirts, crop tops, blazers, and colorful high-heeled pumps—yet, as Michaela had put it, sophisticated and rich.

"Every bad boy from every borough will be at this party," Michaela had said as they rushed into her brand new, candy apple red Mercedes Benz. She had just gotten the car for her seventeenth birthday. The interior was customized with bubblegum pink seats and lavender trim. Gaudy, but signature Michaela.

"Thank God. Because our school is filled with nothing but nerds and wannabes," Paige had replied, pulling down the pink visor so she could use the tiny mirror to coat her lips with a fresh layer of hot pink Chanel lipstick—another Michaela thing. "Even our so-called varsity teams are filled with nerds. Ugh."

"Tell me about it. I would never date anyone at Riverdale. I'm so ready to do something to get kicked out," Michaela groaned. "Maybe I'll set Mrs. Schwartz's hair on fire by accident during lab."

Paige laughed just thinking about their chemistry teacher's dry, frizzy red hair going up in flames. "You better not. You'll be kicked out and arrested. And, there's no way I'd survive without you. I couldn't imagine life without you."

As soon as Michaela and Paige arrived on Fordham Road, Paige knew they were a long way from their sheltered world in Riverdale. They may have both lived in the Bronx, but they lived differently. Paige stared out of the car windows with her mouth hanging slightly open.

Unlike the spaced-out mansions in her neighborhood, these tall apartment buildings held more people on one floor than her entire block did. They looked like someone had stacked bricks randomly and hoped for the best. Lights flickered on and off like there couldn't be too many on all at once.

"Welcome to the real BX," Michaela whispered. "This is the fun part of town." She laughed.

"You mean the dangerous part of town," Paige whispered back. She didn't laugh.

Paige's wide eyes darted around and took in the scene. There were so many people crowded outside, some drinking from bottles covered with brown paper bags, some smoking and passing their brown cigarettes to the person next to them, some throwing dice against the curb and cursing once the dice landed. But, what had struck Paige the most were the girls. There were several huddles of them. One cluster almost the exact clone of the next. They all wore the biggest earrings dangling from their ears and the shortest, tightest skirts Paige had ever seen on young girls. And, she'd never, ever, seen fishnet stockings, except on women on television in those 80s movies she and Michaela liked to watch and laugh at. The girls were loud, and their body language was flirtatious. If it weren't for their baby faces, Paige would have pegged them for prostitutes like the ones she had seen in those movies.

Paige looked over Michaela. "Obviously we are not dressed for this. Do you see that girl's nails? They look like neon green claws, while we're wearing boring French manicures. Way off, Michaela."

"I know, which means we will stand out. Don't you know anything? Look at them," Michaela said and jerked her chin at the girls. "The boys are used to them. Just look how they're trying to get attention, and the boys are all ignoring them. They won't be used to us, which means they'll be all over us. Now come on and stop being scared."

As soon as Paige and Michaela walked into the packed party, Paige started coughing. The thick, gray haze of smoke mixed with cheap colognes and drugstore perfumes was enough to require a gas mask. It didn't faze Michaela.

"Look, but don't be obvious. Ahead . . . 2 o'clock," Michaela yelled in Paige's ear over the booming music.

"What? Another bunch of boys?" Paige asked.

"No, silly! *These* boys are from Wings Academy, the number-one-ranked high school basketball team in the nation," Michaela corrected. "They are future stars!"

Paige shrugged. Neither she nor Michaela needed to be worried about snagging a basketball star. Both of them came from wealthy families. There would be several fifteen-hundred-dollar-per-plate social events their parents would drag them to where they'd be expected to find their future husbands, and they would definitely not be high school basketball players with dreams of being rich. They'd already be rich, from birth.

"Are you crazy, Paige? I hear basketball star dick is the best," Michaela said, pumping her pelvis in and out so Paige would understand.

"Ew. Stop. Just stop." Paige shook her head.

"Virgin," Michaela teased, waving at her.

They laughed.

"No, but seriously, Paige, one of them is looking over here," Michaela had pointed out. "He seems like the star. Look at the girls over there pointing at him. Maybe he wants me."

Paige had already spotted him. Michaela was wrong. For once, a boy was staring at Paige and not Michaela. Paige had felt his eyes on her as soon as she'd waved her vision clear of the thick smoke fog. He was so tall it was hard not to notice him. Even in the dark room, Paige had also noticed that he was teenage-movie-star handsome.

"He's coming this way!" Michaela shouted and bounced like she was about to see her favorite celebrity heartthrob. "Is my hair okay?"

Paige blinked a few times, trying to get her eyes to focus, but within seconds the handsome stranger was standing in front of her. No time to primp or even make sure her hair was okay.

"You want to dance?" he asked, his voice deep with unexpected bass.

Paige's heart throttled upward until she felt like it was caught in her throat. She opened her mouth, but no sound would come out.

Michaela pushed Paige forward before she could answer. "Yes, she does."

"I'm Antonio," he said, holding out his hand.

"Pa . . . Paige," she replied, putting her hand into his.

If Antonio remembered the day that he and Michaela met, he would have to think about how he ended up at that party in the first place. Growing up in the Patterson Houses meant that Antonio actively tried to stay away from functions big enough to cause problems, but his boy, Rich, had insisted.

"Deadass, G, there's going to be so many fine bitches," Rich had said as Antonio laid on his couch earlier that night. He had just finished practice and was more concerned with making sure he got up early enough to hit the gym again in the morning.

"Man, chill, no one cares about that. You not fucking anyway," Antonio said, grabbing the remote off the couch and turning on the T.V.

Rich moved to the set and turned it off. They had been friends for so long, he had spent so much time in Antonio's living room that he didn't even have to look to do it. While Rich didn't grow up in the same projects that Antonio did, he always found his way around and kept Antonio from getting his ass beat every time he curved the gang members who tried to recruit him.

"Well we sure as hell not fucking here, either," Rich said. "May as well up our chances." He smiled in the mischievous way that Antonio recognized meant that he was about to make a dumbass decision, and he was going to take him down with him. Antonio sighed.

"Fuck it, let's go."

Rich and Antonio got to the party twenty minutes before Michaela and Paige did. Like most parties that Rich peer-pressured his friend into going to, the function on Fordham Road was the usual cross between teenage gang bangers trying to sell to the kids from the high schools in the area and the kids from out in Riverdale who thought it would be cute to slum it for a minute. When Rich first saw Michaela and Paige, he knew what category they belonged to, and as he saw his friend's eyes land on Paige and stay there, he snapped his fingers in front of his eyes.

"Yo, nah, don't do that," said Rich. "Ain't nothing over there that you want." He grabbed Antonio's chin and tried to tear his gaze away from what he knew were just two bougie bitches trying to spice up their typical Friday night scene. Antonio clicked his tongue and hit his hand away.

"Boy, don't touch me," Antonio said and turned his eyes back onto the pretty girl who looked like she was trying to go to a business meeting. Rich rolled his eyes. He knew Antonio's type.

"Just because you like to pretend you're not from here doesn't mean they will," he said under his breath, and Antonio, who had actually heard him, ignored it. But that's when Frank, one of those dudes who had dropped out of school at fourteen and looked the part, came to stand in between Antonio and his target for the night.

"What's good?" Frank said to Antonio and Rich, which was bold considering everyone in the neighborhood knew that Antonio didn't entertain delinquency. No one seemed to understand why it was that Antonio was so actively trying to avoid being caught up. It wasn't like it was uncommon for people to sell or to smoke or to do any number of illicit activities. To everyone else, it looked like Antonio just thought he was better than them, that just because he could hoop meant he was something special. But to Antonio, it was more than that.

Even though he didn't know a lot about his father, Antonio knew that he must have been a stand-up dude the way his mother talked about him, the way she kept his name out of her mouth unlike the other single mothers on their block. And because of this, he decided he would keep his head up and out of the streets, no matter how bad things got, or how much money he and his mom went without. He knew in his heart one day his skills with the ball would pay off.

"Get the fuck on, Frank," said Rich. He knew about Antonio's deep disregard for gang life, and even though he found Antonio's fronting annoying sometimes, he supported his friend first. Frank laughed, having expected that reaction, and walked away, bringing Paige back into Antonio's eye line.

"She's breathtaking," Antonio told Rich quietly, not even noticing that her friend was whispering in her ear while staring in their direction.

"You're mad corny. Just go talk to her. You look creepy starting at her like that," said Rich.

Antonio shook his shoulders out and smoothed his eyebrows, and then he crossed the room toward what he now realized were two girls and not one. He could handle women the way he handled a basketball: with delicate finesse before making his shot. As he stood in front of her and looked down, he noticed how pretty her eyes were.

"You want to dance?"

***

Without realizing it, Antonio said the words from his memory out loud, and Paige blinked a few times, remembering where she was. The wedding ceremony was a blur. It was not until cheers erupted from the small crowd of sixty guests that Paige realized it was done. She'd married Antonio for the second time. To hell with the reasons they had divorced in the first place. The reasons . . . Thinking about the reasons made Paige think of Michaela, whose absence at the wedding was as noticeable as a huge sinkhole in the middle of the widely traveled road.

Paige felt sick, but still, she flashed a smile.

"And now I can kiss my bride," Antonio beamed, playing his role. Paige welcomed his tongue into her mouth for a long, passionate seal of their vows. It didn't matter what she felt. She knew it would make for better headlines in the media. Better ratings, too. It would also set her in-laws at ease. Remarrying Antonio needed to solve their problems. It needed to save their lives. It needed to right all of the wrongs. It needed to keep her from having to testify against him . . . them.

Antonio and Paige pulled apart and turned toward their spectators. Cheers arose. Paige's cheeks flushed, and the bones in her face ached from grinning. She deserved an Academy Award.

Antonio wore a cool grin as they slowly made their way down the aisle. He squeezed Paige's hand as if to say, "at least this part is over."

"Wait right there . . . hold that pose!" the photographer called out. "Kiss her," he instructed, hoisting his camera to eye level to ensure he captured the exact moment their lips met. The flash exploded around them. Cameras rolled. Money shot after money shot was captured. This was great.

Paige and Antonio turned to each other on cue, their tongues engaged in another scandalously intimate dance. The photographer's flash lit up in front of them like heavenly beams of light, and the crowd erupted in another round of cheers. Perfection.

The sun basked the couple in abundant light and warmth. It was truly the perfect May afternoon for an outdoor wedding. If only everything else in their lives were this perfect.

"Walk slowly forward now," the photographer instructed, the camera crew backing up for the wide angled shots.

When Paige and Antonio finally made it to the end of the aisle, they were bombarded by guests eager to snap photos with cell phones and personal cameras. Noticing the paparazzi disguised as regular guests, Antonio waved like a politician and Paige flashed her debutante smile. Everyone wanted to get the story first.

"Antonio." Jackson Cartwright stepped into their path, clapping his hand on Antonio's shoulder.

Paige's smile faded, and she bit down into her jaw.

"I didn't think you'd go through with it. I'm proud of you. Maybe you're braver than I thought," Jackson said, smiling. He turned his attention to Paige. "Congratulations."

Paige shivered.

"One more!" the photographer shouted, jutting his camera forward for a close-up.

Paige twisted away, happy for the distraction. Antonio and Paige faced each other, their fake happiness hanging over them like a freshly blown bubble. He kissed her chastely on the nose. She giggled at his playfulness. What a performance! Paige pictured them standing hand-in-hand on a stage, accepting a Tony Award for best actor and actress.

"Antonio!" a voice boomed.

Paige's head whipped left, then right. It was hard to determine what direction the voice had come from until it sounded again. This time, louder. More sinister.

Antonio's head jerked to the left. Paige craned her neck, but there were so many people in front of them.

"Antonio!" the voice boomed again. "You should've played by the rules!" Screams erupted as the wedding goers saw the source of the voice first.

"Oh my God! Gun! He's got a gun!" a guest screamed.

Antonio's eyes widened. Frantically, he unhooked his arm from Paige's and stepped in front of her. Before he could make another move, the sound of rapid-fire explosions cut through the air.

Chapter 1

Fool's Gold

One year earlier

Paige nodded at the hostess and attempted a smile. "Broadwell party," she huffed. She exhaled and tucked her hair behind her left ear. She could feel the perspiration tickling her top lip, but wiping it would smear her freshly beat face. There was no meeting the ladies without a flawless face of makeup.

Paige shifted her weight on her heels as the hostess scanned her list.

"It should be under Michaela Broadwell. I'm kind of late." Paige craned her neck to see if she spotted Michaela in the restaurant, so she could save the hostess some time and point Michaela out.

"Ah, yes. Broadwell. Party of four," the hostess sang like she'd just discovered something great. "Right this way."

Paige followed, rehearsing believable excuses in her head.

Sorry girl, but just as I was walking out, Christian got sick.

Girl, blame my mother. She called with her usual melodrama, and I lost track of time listening to her complain.

Sorry to have you waiting. The nanny called out, and I had to get a sitting service last minute.

Paige could live with picking one of those excuses—anything other than the real reason she was late. She could imagine the slight hint of satisfaction masked as concern that would crop up on Michaela's face if she knew what really happened. Paige envisioned Michaela sucking in her breath and her cat-green eyes going round. "Oh, Paige. I'm so sorry this is happening to you," Michaela would say sympathetically, as if Paige had just told her she had cancer. Paige swallowed hard. That would make her sick. She hated people to pity her.

Paige loved Michaela, but they'd always had a mildly competitive relationship. As kids, if Paige got a new bike, Michaela would beg her parents for a bigger, prettier, fancier bike. As teens, if Paige got a new piece of jewelry from her father, like the diamond tennis bracelet she got at her sweet sixteen, Michaela would be sure to get the bracelet, earrings, and necklace. Even as adults, when Paige's relationship with Antonio got serious, Michaela killed herself to find an athlete who could measure up, though Michaela's mother had wanted her to marry Barry Richardson, a future lawyer whose parents were wealthy.

All of that aside, Paige loved Michaela. Paige couldn't imagine her life without Michaela. Without her, who would she tell her deepest secrets? Who would give her advice? Who would be her voice when she lost hers, which was often? Michaela always had Paige's back, and even when social anxiety kept Paige from speaking up for herself in certain situations, Michaela would step in and be her mouthpiece.

"Here we are," the hostess said, extending her hand toward the seat like a church usher. "I'll leave the menu here for you. Enjoy ladies."

"Thank you," Paige huffed, plunking her bag down in the empty chair next to hers.

Before she could sit down, Michaela was on her. "Thank you for gracing me with your presence, Mrs. Roberts," Michaela sniped, tapping the top of her sparkly, diamond-encrusted Rolex, another "out-do Paige" item.

"I know. I know."

"You know, alright. You know I do not like looking like a chick on a blind date that got stood up," Michaela complained with the strained chuckle that meant she was annoyed but trying. She stood up, and they exchanged a perfunctory hug and cheek-to-cheek air kiss.

Michaela looked beautiful as usual. Paige admired how Michaela kept her skin glowing all year around like she was fresh off of a Caribbean beach vacation every day.

"Just been a crazy day," Paige said, her voice clipped. She didn't bother to offer one of her practiced excuses. Michaela knew her too well.

"You know I wanted to have some time alone with you before the other girls got here." Michaela looked at her watch again. "Shit, now we only have about twenty minutes to chat before the gossip hound and the preacher's wife arrive."

"I'm sorry," Paige said, leaving it at that. She picked up a glass of water with already melted ice and sipped, hoping it would settle her stomach.

"So, what's up, girl?" Paige let Michaela start talking about what was going on with her. That always did the trick when Paige wanted to forget her own problems. Michaela loved to have the spotlight, and Paige loved to give it to her.

"There's so much happening," Michaela lowered her voice and leaned in closer to the table, her green eyes wide like what she had to say was top secret.

Paige uncurled her toes and let her shoulders drop. For the first time in hours, she relaxed. There was always so much happening with Michaela. She would forever be one of those spoiled rich girls who believed every small thing was a huge deal. Michaela could make a garden snake into a boa constrictor, or a campfire into a raging inferno. But, the one thing Paige had always admired about her best friend was her fearlessness. Michaela was fearless in a way that would make her jump in the face of a six-foot-tall hulk of a man in a road rage incident and punch him in the face without blinking an eye.

"So, hurry up and fill me in," Paige urged. Anything to keep Michaela from asking her about what was going on in her life.

"Well, Rod is retiring. But, you already know that. So, I'm in the process of planning the party. I think it'll be good for him. A change. A break from his . . . you know . . . grief."

Paige nodded. She wanted to ask so badly if Michaela really thought right now was a good time in Rod's life for a party. His brother had just been murdered and dragged through the mud as a drug-dealing gangbanger in the media. But the excitement in Michaela's voice made Paige stay silent.

"Oh my God, that party planner—Minted Events—has the best ideas. Shayna, the owner, flew in all the way from Houston just to show me samples of what she has. Now, that's customer service. And, I'm scouring all of the top designers for my dress. It has to be two seasons ahead, or else it simply won't work," Michaela prattled.

Paige nodded and sipped her water. Just envisioning any over-the-top event Michaela would throw made Paige feel like sinking into the floor. She thought she could put her worries aside for this lunch with the ladies, but she hadn't considered that their usual pretentious banter would send her mind racing, worrying. Would she even be able to afford a designer dress for Michaela's husband's retirement party? Who would be there? Would there be a red carpet? Paparazzi? Would everyone know what happened by then?

"I have to find him a suit, because you know Rod. He'll show up in a hoodie and sweats if I don't reel him in. After all these years with this beauty as a wife, he is still like the beast—"

"Antonio got let go from another team." Paige didn't know why, but the words just bubbled out of her. Her stomach contracted. Saying the words gave Paige the kind of relief you felt after vomiting. She gulped her water this time, wishing it were a stiff drink. And she didn't even drink.

Michaela's eyebrows shot up into arches, and she flattened her right hand over her heart. "Oh, Paige. I'm so sorry."

Paige had almost had her words down perfectly.

"He says we'll be okay. They bought out the contract, and he's going to invest the money," Paige said, trying to convince herself, more than Michaela, that her lifestyle would stay the same and that she wouldn't be explaining things to her parents . . . again.

"You don't have to give up your house, do you?" Michaela gasped like she was asking if Paige had to have both of her lungs removed. "And what about Christian . . . will he have to change schools? What about your parents? What will they say? Will you ask them for help? Will you get a job?" Michaela shot questions at her, rapid fire.

Paige blanched. She had already asked herself all of those questions when Antonio came home, half drunk, and woke her with the news. Paige had sat up in the bed, her black velvet sleep mask pulled up on her forehead, and sleep clouding her brain. She listened to Antonio rant about how it had happened this time.

"They were all standing around in Dan's office, all smug and shit," Antonio had griped, sitting at her side, hunched over with his elbows on his knees and his fists clenched.

"Of course Dan hid behind his fancy, big-dog desk like a coward. Couldn't even hold eye contact with me. They acted like I needed a handout or some shit. I played my ass off for that team. Everybody knows I got at least three more good years on the court."

Paige swung her legs over the side of the bed and got closer to him. She'd contemplated hugging him, but didn't.

"Can you believe Dan spoke to me like I was one of those kids who'd tried out for the team but didn't make it? 'Tony, you've been a pleasure to work with. All of us . . . the entire organization has nothing but respect and admiration for you. We think you're a great guy and personally, I think you're one of the best guards I know. But we have to move in a different direction. These young players are a new breed, stronger, faster, and we have to be able to compete,'" Antonio repeated general manager Dan Sidelman's words almost verbatim. When he was done, Antonio moved his tongue over his bottom lip, like uttering the words had left behind a painful, oozing blister.

Paige lowered her eyes to her trembling hands. She wanted to be supportive. For goodness sake, she could see the disappointment hiding behind Antonio's anger. She had also sensed that it was different from the look she had seen Antonio wear every time he'd been traded or let go before. Paige knew it was the end of Antonio's basketball career. She had felt a prickling sense of horror like some dreadful poverty monster would jump out of her closet and snatch her up.

"What will we do?" she'd asked, her fear making her unable to bring herself to hug him or offer any comfort.

Antonio had blown out a windstorm of breath, braced himself, and stood up from the bed. "I'll work it out," he said, rubbing his chin like he always did when he was thinking. "Things aren't going to just fall apart overnight. I'll invest everything I have left and make it grow. I know plenty of people that can help me make money."

Paige had taken in a deep, shaky breath. She hadn't wanted to press. She wasn't the nagging type, but she shuddered at the thought of going through another tough financial time waiting for a team to pick Antonio up. Just thinking about going through that again made the hairs on her neck stand up. Thinking of all of the pretending she would have to do in front of her friends and family was what twisted her insides into knots the most. And her son—he deserved to live like she had as a child.

Paige had looked around her expansive bedroom and wondered how they were going to maintain their lifestyle this time. Would it be an unauthorized loan from her brother's trust fund, again? Would she go behind Antonio's back and ask her mother again? Would she pawn off a few handbags, jewelry? Or would she leave this time?

"That's what you said before, and we almost lost everything," Paige blurted out. She'd wanted to be supportive. She really did. She felt a pang of guilt for saying it, but she didn't take it back. This time, she couldn't back her words.

Antonio tipped his head back and stared at the ceiling with a clenched jaw. "Don't worry, Paige. I won't let you be embarrassed because you can't spend ten thousand dollars on a bag or take a European vacation for two-fucking-weeks. God forbid. I'd rather kill myself first," he shot back.

"Don't take your frustrations out on me, Antonio. This impacts me too. We have a child in private school. Music lessons. Tennis lessons. Rowing. We have this house. And, what about all of the cars? What will people think if we have to downgrade our lifestyle?"

Antonio chortled a deep, guttural sound full of contradiction to the scowl on his face. "Wow. Really, Paige? That's what you're going with?" Antonio said and shook his head in disgust. "Everything you just mentioned was material shit. Every. Single. Thing." He slapped the balled fingers on his right hand into the palm of his left as he said the last three words. "Do you even realize the shit that runs your life? You have no other purpose, do you? Impressing the world—that's it, huh? Like mother, like daughter? Living for what others think of you? No real identity?"

Paige had sprung to her feet, his words a gut-punch. She'd folded her arms across her chest to stave off the ache she felt in her belly.

"What else is there to think about in a time like this? Obviously, all of these years, my purpose has been to make sure you don't fuck up our lives, Antonio. I've stuck by you through things that most women would've bailed out on a long time ago. Remember that. That's love. You never wanted me to work. You never want me to go to my parents for anything. You always want to pretend you've got it. I'm not going to pretend with you this time," Paige had said in her chilliest voice. The gloves had certainly come off. She regretted the words as soon as she'd said them, but it had been too late. She hated being like that with him. And, she knew how sensitive Antonio was about living up to her parent's standards.

"Right, I know. I pretend." Antonio threw his hands up. "Yes, that's it. I pretend that you spend thousands of dollars a month with no regard for where it came from or is coming from. I pretend that your parents are always secretly judging me because no matter how good you live, no matter how much I give you, I will always be that poor kid from the projects that just happened to make it out of the hood . . . never good enough for the senator's daughter, no matter what. I also pretend I don't know you regret losing your trust fund because you fell in love with me. And, most-of-fucking-all, Paige, I pretend that you would've married me even if I wasn't on my way to the League!" Antonio had exploded.

"Stop it! I didn't mean it like that," Paige yelled as tears danced down her flushed cheeks. How had she meant it?

"Look," Antonio had exhaled, softening.

She knew that he hated to see her cry. He hated to disappoint her. He'd said that probably one thousand times during their marriage.

"I said I would work it out, and I will."

"Hey, ladies!" the shrill southern drawl broke up Paige's thoughts and ended Michaela's barrage of what-will-you-do questions.

Michaela's face, which had just a second ago been dragged down with pity for Paige, was suddenly jovial. "Koi! It's so good to see you!"

Paige shifted in her seat at how easy it was for Michaela to change moods. Paige imagined that this talent of Michaela's must've been a gift and a curse.

"Paigey," Koi sang, pushing on Paige's shoulder.

Paige wanted to vomit, but she plastered on a fake smile, pushed away from the table, and stood up.

Let the pretending begin.

"Wait, have you lost weight? Girl, you are so beautiful. The lighting in this place is doing it for those gray eyes," Koi gushed in her annoying sing-songy-Paula-Deen voice. She tapped cheeks with Paige. A real Southern belle.

"I know I say this every time, but you two, with that ashy blond hair, that buttery skin that you both seem to be able to keep so radiant all year 'round, and those colored eyes . . . green and gray is it . . . always make me think of twins . . . sisters, at least," Koi gushed. "Yes, twins. There has to be some family connection. It's just too strange."

Is she going to say that every time she sees us? Paige wondered, annoyed.

People always asked Paige and Michaela if they were sisters, and when they'd say no, they'd ask, "Cousins, at least?"

Paige guessed it was because ignorant people thought it so rare that two black girls, friends no less, could have fair skin, dusty blond hair, and colored eyes.

Paige and Michaela had also discussed Koi's obsession with their looks. Paige opined that Koi was uncomfortable with her own coffee-bean complexion, which she noticeably tried to lighten with the wrong, way-too-light shade of foundation. There was nothing about Koi that Paige really thought was endearing, but she put up with her for the sake of Michaela and to say she had friends. It was just what socialites did—maintain fake friendships, meet and eat, and spend money on things that boosted their reputations.

Every time they met up, Paige thought, *Who named their child Koi?* Wasn't that the name of those hideous orange, red, and silver fish that swam around in the neat little decorative ponds of rich people who thought they brought them good feng shui?

Koi was married to Damien Armstrong, former criminal-turned-pastor of Full of Life Ministries, a megachurch in Westchester. Koi was far from what Paige would've considered first lady-like. Growing up, Paige watched the first lady of her family's church sit quietly in the front pew wearing an angelic smile, dressed in almost floor-length paisley dresses with lace-trimmed collars that covered her collarbone, and she spoke in mousy, hushed murmurs while church members always seemed to be fussing over her. The total opposite of Koi, who never left home in anything other than the brightest, tightest, above-the-knee dresses with so much cleavage-spillage she could probably double as a circus sideshow—the megachurch first lady who could balance a Bible on her breasts. Koi spoke loudly as if she was always on a stage commanding an audience's attention. She lived for attention. And, did first ladies wear so much weave and outlandish clown-like makeup? Today's choice was a purple, glittery eyeshadow and shiny fuchsia lipstick.

At that moment, Paige was a bit annoyed by Koi's presence. She was just another person to make Paige feel like her life was in shambles.

"You know, in all of my years in New York, I've never come to this place. Heard about it, never got around to it. Damien is so busy all the time. With his flock of believers growing each week, date nights have become few and far between," Koi said as she looked around in wide-eyed amazement.

Paige smirked. "I'm surprised. You're so . . . you know . . . worldly, and this place has been around for-ever."

La Grenouille was a well-known celebrity haunt in Manhattan that Michaela always felt was worth making appearances at, so they visited often. Paige loved the rustic, yet modern ambiance. The wooden walls, the traditional furniture that still looked new, the bouquets of fresh flowers, and classic light fixtures gave the inside of the restaurant a suave, chic feel.

"I love it here. Caught quite a few juicy news tidbits in this place," Casey announced, approaching from the side like she'd been part of the conversation all along.

Paige, Michaela, and Koi all seemed to look up at the same time with simultaneous raised-brow, mouth-agape surprise.

"Hey girls," Casey sang. "How did y'all know exactly where to sit? This is my favorite table. This is the perfect spot. Front and center. I can enjoy and still see if any celebrities bounce in on the creep. You all know I love a good, juicy story."

"It's so rude to sneak up on people," Michaela grumbled at Casey without bothering to stand up. Koi gave Casey a weak air kiss and a flat, "Hey, girl." Paige stood and gave Casey a tight hug.

Michaela sighed heavily and picked up her menu. Paige shot her a stern look. She was starting to believe that Michaela was jealous of her friendship with Casey.

"We haven't ordered anything while we waited for you. I'm starving, so can you sit down," Michaela griped with a passive aggressive smile.

"I sure can," Casey replied, overly cheery. She pulled out the chair next to Paige.

Michaela exhaled loudly.

Casey's arrival made Paige feel better. Someone normal, finally. Casey didn't have it as good financially as they all did, but she had become a good source of information since she was one of the most popular gossip bloggers on the web, and Paige thought she was more genuine than most of the women in the social elite of the New York City scene. There was something pure about Casey that Paige couldn't quite place, but it was endearing just the same. Paige didn't know if it was Casey's deep cheek dimples, which made her look like an innocent-faced baby cherub, or if it was that Casey didn't care to pretend like they all did. Casey was full figured and was never one to eat bird food or pretend she was trying to lose weight.

Casey also wasn't as materialistic and showy as the rest of them. Casey proudly rocked her Michael Kors bags, when the others wouldn't be caught dead with Michael Kors anything. Paige admired that a man didn't define Casey. Casey made her own money from her celebrity gossip blog and the burgeoning online boutique for big girls that she owned. She lived by her own rules and was always proud to say that she was single and ready to mingle—a luxury Paige had never been afforded, since she'd given herself solely to Antonio since high school.

Michaela and Paige had had a few spats over Paige's friendship with Casey. Paige had put Michaela in her place once. "I don't know what you have against this girl. Just because you don't know what it is like to be new to any situation, no friends, no support, doesn't mean everyone is like you. Give her a chance. She's smart and independent. We could learn a thing or two from her," Paige had chided.

"So, what's good on the menu?" Koi asked as she scanned her leather-bound menu like it was hard to read.

"I like everything. You can't go wrong in classy restaurants," Michaela replied without looking up from her menu.

"Good evening, ladies," a tall, slender, handsome young waiter approached. "I'm Anwar, and I'll be serving you this evening."

"Mmm. An-war." Koi licked her lips and sized him up. "I can appreciate a young prince named after an African leader," Koi said, pushing up her already bulging cleavage.

Paige wanted to throw her water on Koi to cool her down. Again, more un-first-lady-like behavior.

"I'll start with a Cosmo," Michaela ordered first.

"Hennessy sidecar for me," Koi went next.

A first lady drinking Hennessy?

"For me . . . something light and fruity. I don't drink," Paige said.

"My usual, Anwar," Casey chimed in, winking at the waiter.

Michaela sucked her teeth, and Koi grunted. Paige lowered her head and smiled.

By the time the food came, all of the ladies had loosened up. Even Paige had forgotten her fight with Antonio for the time being. In some strange way, the chatter, the ebb and flow of stomach-hurting laughter, and even the masked bitchiness and blatant competitiveness that hovered over the table, brought Paige some comfort. She'd looked around at every single one of her friends and thought, at that moment, she was like fool's gold, all shiny and believable on the surface, when deep down she felt fake and worthless.

"Okay, okay listen," Casey slurred a bit, the result of four drinks, and clapped her hands together. "I can't keep this in another minute."

Paige stopped mid-bite to listen. Michaela rolled her eyes. Koi kept shoveling the restaurant's famous crab cakes into her mouth like she'd never eaten out in her life.

"I have some news," Casey said mysteriously.

"Okay?" Michaela replied, tilting her head to the side.

Casey had everyone's attention. They all knew she was the Information Queen. When Casey had news, everyone had better listen.

Paige could see the slight tinge of nervousness creep into everyone's features. Would Casey's news be some sordid story about one of their famous husbands?

"We . . . meaning all of us BFFs here," Casey continued, darting her big, Betty Boop eyes around from face to face and hesitating like a game show host drawing heart-pounding suspense before the announcement of the grand prize.

Michaela kicked Paige under the table.

Paige gave her a crinkled-brow, motherly look that meant, "Be nice."

"We have been offered our own reality show!" Casey cheered, fanning her hands in front of her and bouncing in her seat. "Mina Lacks-Yousef, the mega-producer of all things reality T.V., wants us to join her Rich Wives franchise! We would be the Rich Wives of the Bronx."

Koi's fork hitting the plate was the only sound at the table. Paige quickly picked up the fruity drink Anwar had brought out earlier and threw it back so fast she didn't even taste it. There would be no more nursing that drink. Michaela's usually slanted eyes went round.

Casey looked around at their faces. "I know, right? Isn't this good news?" Casey asked with jolly confidence. "I mean, let's face it, this would be a golden opportunity for everyone here. I could use the exposure to broaden my platform, and I'm sure my boutique will be exploding with orders," she said, touching her chest proudly. She turned sideways to face Koi. "And you . . . Oh my goodness, you can finally get out from under Damien's shadow and have a camera crew following his sneaky butt at the same time. We know his reputation with the ladies."

Koi blinked, dumbfounded like she was thinking, *What reputation with the ladies?*

Casey faced Michaela now. "Michaela, we all know how you love to show off, right? And, with Rod retiring from football, you'll need something else to keep you relevant on the social scene. . . ."

Michaela opened her mouth to clap back, but Casey kept on speaking.

"And, Paige. Girl, you know you're my favorite. This would be just perfect for you. You need to come out of that little shell you live in. Get your own sense of self. I mean, with Antonio's basketball career being over and no trust fund from the great Senator Gladstone, you'll be able to keep things afloat this time."

A collective gasp flitted over the table. Suddenly, all eyes were on Paige.

Paige's color drained, and suddenly she was filled with a nauseating wave of disbelief. It was another punch from reality. She shot up from her chair and staggered slightly.

"Paige! Wait!" Casey called after her. She turned back to the women at the table. "What? What did I say? Didn't everyone already know?" Casey asked, her eyes big and genuine. "Does this mean she won't be on the show?"

Chapter 2

Real Life

Paige turned around twice and opened her arms like she was making a snow angel in the air.

"That's the one. That is definitely the one," Michaela said.

"Are you sure?" Paige asked, letting her arms fall at her side as she turned to the mirror and looked at herself in the emerald green gown one last time. "I've never worn Carolina Herrera's lower end line. I don't want to seem like a snob, but . . ."

"First of all, Paige, you are a snob. Second of all, would I tell you it was the one if it wasn't?" Michaela replied, rolling her eyes. "How long have we been friends? Ugh."

"Okay. I'll take your word for it," Paige said, walking back into the fitting room. "Come get it."

Michaela sighed and snatched the dress over the fitting room door. She tossed it on top of the huge pile the tiny salesgirl held on her arms.

"What about shoes?" Paige called out as she put back on her clothes.

Michaela rolled her eyes again. "Remind me not to come shopping with you again, Paige. You'd think I know better after almost twenty-two years. Do like me, hire a personal shopper. They bring everything to your house, and you can sit in your parlor with tea and crumpets and pick out what you want."

"You're the one who picked a yoga class right on Fifth Avenue," Paige said as she emerged from the fitting room, still fixing her clothes. "You're also the one who can't pass a Neiman Marcus without running inside to see if your personal shopper got everything that's out for the season. I would've never stopped today if you didn't say to. Especially not with yoga pants on and messy buns."

Michaela touched the dusty-blond pile of hair in the middle of her head. "Shit, you're right."

Paige raised a brow and nodded at Michaela as if to say, "Remember whose idea this was in the first place."

"It was supposed to be five minutes, remember?" Paige reminded. "Better hope we don't run into anyone we know. Now, pipe down, I'm almost done." Paige chuckled. "Besides, you sound like my mother. Tea and crumpets? Really?"

Michaela threw her hand up to her chest like she was clutching her pearls. "Please don't send me to the hospital. Me, sound like Lillian Tillary, oh my God. Gag me with a spoon, why don't you?"

They laughed.

"Let's get out of here." Paige signaled the salesgirl. "I'm ready to check out." The tiny girl craned her neck to see behind the pile of clothes and smiled.

"How is old, stuffy Lillian these days, anyway?" Michaela asked as they stood at the counter while the salesgirl rang up the purchases.

Paige scoffed. "Do you really need to ask? She's still the same: supportive, yet bossy. Busy, yet bored. Keeping up appearances and trying to impress my grandmother is still her life goal. My mother won't ever change."

"And Mr. G?"

"Daddy is the same too. Busy with his 'special projects,'" Paige replied, using air quotes. "He joked at dinner last week about running for president. He takes this 'tough on crime' crap too far sometimes." Paige rolled her eyes. "He better not even try it. The country already said there was only room for one black president."

"Well, your daddy ain't exactly black," Michaela said, rubbing the inside of her palm.

"Shut up." Paige swatted at her.

"I'm just saying," Michaela chuckled. "You know how us light-skinned Negros get by."

Paige laughed. "You're a mess."

"That'll be six thousand, two hundred and fifty-six dollars, and thirty-three cents," the salesgirl interrupted with a smile.

"Can you imagine, my father, President of the United States?" Paige rambled as she dug into her Louis Vuitton duffle that doubled as her yoga bag and pulled out her wallet. "I thought the spotlight of being a senator's daughter was bad, but that would be ridiculous." She mindlessly handed the salesgirl her credit card and turned her attention back to Michaela.

"Can't even imagine," Michaela agreed. "I take my wig, hat, and my whole damn scalp off to Michelle Obama. I couldn't be her and remain that composed, girl. And those two beautiful brown girls of theirs, having to live under all of that scrutiny. Too much."

"Right!" Paige replied. "Michelle is the queen of keeping it together."

"Well, what about you?" Michaela asked. "You know . . . the situation."

Paige knew Michaela had been waiting for the opportunity to ask about her and Antonio's financial situation. Ever since the day in the restaurant, the topic had been pulling between them like a tug of war rope.

"We're just fine. It's like nothing has changed. Antonio has been meeting with people and taking care of things. He's made some pretty good, sound investments." As Paige said the words, a cold chill shot down her back. The truth was, Paige had been afraid to ask. She and Antonio had been living like nothing had happened in the weeks since he'd gotten cut. Her lifestyle hadn't changed much at all. Not that she could tell anyway.

"I knew Antonio would take care of it," Michaela said confidently. "He is not going to let anything come between him and his Paigey Poo."

Paige shrugged. There it was again. Michaela had always had an unwavering faith in Antonio since he and Paige had met. She was like his secret cheerleader, and even when he was wrong in Paige's eyes, Michaela would always convince Paige to see things from Antonio's point-of-view. She'd always end her Antonio advocacy with, "Remember: good men are hard to find and they all have faults. Hold on to him. Somebody else would gladly snatch him up."

"He said he would. I'm trying to believe that. It hasn't been easy pretending that I'm not worried," Paige replied.

"I've considered doing the show," Michaela said, seemingly off topic. "What about you? If I did it, would you?"

Paige twisted her lips. "I don't know. That's not for me. I don't think I'd like to live my life in the spotlight any more than I have," she said, though she had considered it as a means of having her own income for once in her life. She shook her head. "I don't think my marriage would survive reality TV. What about Rod? Is he fine with you doing the show?"

"Psh," she waved. "Rod doesn't care. He's not like Antonio. My feelings don't matter all that much. Probably never did."

"You sure? The last time we all got together, you both seemed to be in a better place. Although, I didn't think he'd even want a party after . . . you know . . . the thing with his brother."

Michaela shuddered. "Rod is a strong man. He'll survive. At some point, he'll have to snap out of it. He will have to get control of his emotions, or else." She shrugged, her tone evasive and unsure.

"What does that—" Paige began.

"I'm sorry, ma'am," the salesgirl interrupted, wearing a painful expression.

Paige turned in the girl's direction, her head tilted.

"The card you provided didn't go through," the salesgirl said, her voice mousy and sorrowful.

"Impossible," Paige said evenly. "Try it again. It has to be your machine."

"I . . . um . . . I tried it three times. That's all I'm allowed."

Heat crept up Paige's body until the tops of her ears burned. She hated to be embarrassed.

"That's crazy. I guess maybe the strip got damaged? I have other cards." She dug into her wallet and handed the girl another card.

"That's an American Express Centurion card, or what you might call a Black Card. Meaning no limit," Paige said, an annoyed edge in her voice. Now she had something to prove. But to who? Herself? Michaela? This little girl she didn't even know?

Paige could feel Michaela watching. She knew what Michaela was thinking, but she was wrong. In the weeks since Antonio had been let go, he'd made some major investments. Paige hadn't asked to see proof. But, he said they would be fine.

"Yes, ma'am," the salesgirl said, reaching out with a shaky hand to take Paige's card.

Paige turned toward Michaela. "Can't be my card. That would be ridiculous."

"Exactly," Michaela agreed, glaring at the poor salesgirl like she purposely declined the card. That's what good friends did: pretend with you.

"Unfortunately, ma'am, this card also declined," the girl said, daring not to make eye contact with Paige this time.

Paige's entire body became engulfed in heat like she'd been ignited with gasoline and a match. She could almost feel her chest heaving, and she got that noodle-like feeling in her legs again.

"Impossible," her voice rose, garnering the attention of other store patrons. "Do you know who I am?"

We still have money. I am not broke.

The salesgirl put her hands up and hunched her shoulders, a gesture of confusion and apology all in one.

"Call over a manager," Michaela insisted. "You must be new, but we're not."

"I assure you both, I did everything right," the salesgirl replied, a bit of defiance in her voice now that they were asking for a manager.

"We'll determine that with your manager present." Michaela leaned in closer to the counter. "Go. Go on. Get a manager." Michaela flicked her hand at the girl.

Paige shook her head. "This is crazy. I'll never come back in here again."

"That personal shopper is sounding good right about now, huh?" Michaela joked, trying to make light of the situation.

"Let's just go," Paige said. However, the manager approached before they could turn to leave.

The manager, an older woman with silver hair pushed back in a bun so tight it gave her an automatic facelift, rushed over, wearing a strained smile. She stood behind the counter where Paige's bags were neatly lined up.

"Hi, I'm Margaret," the manager sang, forcing a smile to stay in place like she already knew what to expect here. "Christina told me she's tried two cards, both three times each, and—"

"And, she doesn't know what she's doing," Michaela interjected, stepping in front of Paige. "This is Paige Tillary Roberts, wife of NBA star Antonio Roberts and daughter of prominent senator Gladstone Tillary. She has money. There's no way her cards are declined. I've known her all my—"

"Those cards were working fine yesterday," Paige finally spoke up, feeble, compared to Michaela's forceful tone. "Matter of fact, to clear up any confusion, here. This is my debit card," Paige handed the manager another card with a Visa logo. "It's linked to my bank account, so I know it will go through." Paige bit down into her jaw, hoping she wasn't wrong.

Margaret took the card, cleared her throat, and nodded.

Paige's stomach twisted, her knees knocked, and sweat beads ran a race down her back. She hadn't felt lightheaded like this since she'd fainted at a social tea before she knew she was pregnant with Christian.

Margaret looked up from the register, sorrow etched into her expression like she was about to announce that someone had died. "Mrs. Roberts, I . . . just . . . I'm . . . I'm sorry." She held all three cards out toward Paige. "You may want to contact your financial institution. Store policy forbids me from trying any more of your cards." Margaret pulled the shopping bags down from the glass counter and set them behind her, out of Paige and Michaela's reach.

"Oh my God," Michaela huffed. "Now she's acting like we are going to snatch and run. Ridiculous. We don't call banks like people who watch our pennies, okay? I'll pay for the shit. If my cards don't go through, I'll know it's the damn machines in here." Michaela went to dig into her Chanel knapsack.

"No," Paige grabbed Michaela's wrist. "Just forget it. I have plenty of things to wear. I was just being lazy anyway. I'm not going to argue with these people."

"You sure?" Michaela asked. "You're my girl. You know it's nothing. I know you got it, Paige. You can pay me back later."

Paige's face was on fire and both of her temples throbbed. "I know. But, it's okay. Let's just go," she said, pulling Michaela forward. "You and I both know I didn't need one damn thing that was in those bags."

As they exited Neiman Marcus, Paige was preoccupied with getting away from Michaela and the store. She cringed when she remembered she rode to yoga in Michaela's car. Paige bit down on her bottom lip, her mind racing. Had someone stolen her identity? She didn't really want to ask her friend to drive her straight to her bank, but the declined cards were burning a hole in Paige's soul. There was no way their money could've disappeared that fast.

"Maybe I should stop at my bank," she spoke up, finally breaking the uncomfortable silence in Michaela's Range

Rover. "What if my identity was compromised? I'd need to know that right away."

Michaela shook her head. "You know, I was just thinking that same thing. One of these scamming lowlifes out here probably compromised your cards. These banks don't play. They act fast. Yes. I know it. That is exactly what happened."

"Yes, I think so too," Paige murmured.

Paige and Michaela had been doing this deflection dance during embarrassing or uncomfortable moments for years. It had preserved their friendship whenever things got tense. If there was a topic too hard to talk about, one of them would find a rationalization for what was happening, and the other would simply go along with it to ease the tension of the moment.

"Straight to the bank we go," Michaela said, whipping her SUV in the opposite direction.

Paige crossed then re-crossed her legs and swung the right one in and out. It felt like she'd been waiting for an eternity.

"Paige?" Latrice Crane, one of the bank's managers, sang with a friendly smile.

Paige stood up. "Hi, Latrice. I need to speak to you. I just went through something crazy. I think my accounts have been compromised." Paige let the words spill from her mouth like holding them in any longer would choke her to death.

"Um . . . come to my office, Paige."

Something about Latrice's soft, mournful tone made Paige's stomach churn. She felt like she was being led to the glass window at the morgue to identify a dead loved one. It was almost like Latrice was expecting her.

"Have a seat." Latrice closed the door and pulled the blinds down on the glass window that looked out into the bank, while Paige settled into an armchair in front of her desk.

"I went to buy something today. A relatively small purchase, just over six thousand dollars, and every one of my cards was declined," Paige blurted, getting to the point.

Latrice sighed as she made her way past Paige and took her seat in front of her computer. "I thought you knew what was going on, Paige. I assumed that Antonio would've spoken to you." She pecked at her keyboard and squinted at her computer screen.

"What do you mean?"

Latrice turned her full attention to Paige. She laced her fingers together in front of her.

"Paige, Antonio came in earlier today and cleared out all of the accounts. Again, I assumed with something like that, he would have spoken to you, and that it was a decision made by you both."

"I am joint on those accounts. He would need my permission to close them."

"Actually, Paige, Antonio changed that months ago. You were a cardholder, but he took you off as account signatory."

Paige's ears rang like tiny bombs had exploded around her. She moved to the edge of the chair. She felt like someone had her in a headlock, squeezing so hard she was about to suffocate.

"My family has been banking here forever. In fact, my father was the one who helped get this Black-owned bank recognized nationally, so what would make you think I would want to close the accounts? Why wouldn't someone contact me for proof?" Paige found her voice. She used the only defense she had. She'd been leaning on her family's reputation and her father's influence all her life. It was lame, but it was all she had at that moment.

"I'm really sorry, Paige. You'll have to speak with Antonio."

Paige's jaw shifted in and out, back and forth. "Talk to Antonio? I'm talking to you. I know that everyone around here feels loyalty to Antonio because of his endorsement deal with this bank, but I think it's high time you and your little groupie coworkers remember who brought Antonio and his big NBA checks to this bank. My family has been banking here for generations. There are a lot of businesses that bank here because of my father and grandfather. One call from my father and they would all follow him right across the street to Spring Bank." There it was again. The threat of her family, Paige's only defense mechanism. Paige wasn't herself. She was more like Michaela. The feeling of losing control like this made her dizzy. She wanted to throw herself on the floor and kick and scream and cry.

Latrice cleared her throat. The exhausted look on her face said that she was used to Paige subliminally accusing her and her coworkers of lusting after Antonio. Latrice let it roll off of her shoulder as she usually did. "Paige, I know what your family means to this bank. I have great respect for your father, and my loyalties are always with him. I know you're upset. I'm not supposed to give out this information, but I'll tell you."

The scowl on Paige's face softened a bit. She was suddenly embarrassed about her previous outburst.

"Two hours ago, Bernard helped Antonio, and what he told me matches the activity on your accounts. Antonio made several large wire transfers from each account and withdrew the rest in cash and cashier's checks. Usually, with that kind of rush activity, it means something is terribly wrong. It's been my experience that account holders who do that are hiding assets. Trying to recover from something drastic. If I were you, I'd have a talk with him right away. I understand how alarming this is. I am truly sorry, but there's nothing else I can do."

Paige swallowed hard. Her heart throttled up, and her mind raced. She stood up on wobbly legs, feeling like her shame was emblazoned on her chest like a scarlet letter. "Thank you for your help, Latrice. I'm . . . I apologize."

Latrice put her hand up and smiled. "No need to apologize. Like I said, I can imagine how unnerving this must be."

Oh, you have no fucking idea!

"Is everything okay?" Michaela asked before Paige could fully get into the passenger's seat of her SUV.

"It was just what we suspected. Someone compromised my accounts," Paige lied.

"Well, what did they say?"

"They're changing everything and sending me all new cards."

"Oh goodness. I can't imagine that happening to me. I would've died if I was ever in a store and my cards declined. The thought of it is like my worst nightmare."

Paige fell silent. There was no way she could tell Michaela the truth.

"The entire ordeal has given me a headache. Do you mind picking up Christian when you get Chloe?"

"C'mon, girl. You know that is no problem. I'll pick him up and keep him for the night. You go home and rest."

"Thanks, girl. This means the world."

"Oh and . . . just think about that opportunity to be on the show. I think your storyline would be perfect. Especially now."

Paige wasn't focused on reality TV; she was focused on her real life.

Paige rushed through the doors of her home as if her life depended on finding something inside.

"Ms. Roberts," Catalina, the housekeeper stated.

Paige threw her hand up. "Not now, Lina. Not now."

Paige took the winding staircase two steps at a time. Her heart thrashed against her sternum, and she could hardly breathe. Her lips were painfully dry from breathing through her mouth. She rushed through the French doors of her bedroom and paused. She took a deep, shaky breath as she stared over at Antonio's side of the bed. Catalina had already made it up. Paige rushed to his nightstand and yanked open the drawer. Nail clipper, cigar cutter, old condoms (she'd made him wear them for a while after. . .), and a wallet-sized picture of Christian. Nothing seemed different. Paige whirled around, trying to see if anything else seemed out of place. Everything seemed perfect. The dreadful thought that he'd packed up and left had trampled through her mind on her way home and sent her into a panic. Why else would he clean out all of their money without telling her? They'd argued, sure, but that was weeks ago. Paige had settled on Antonio's word that he was taking care of things. What had changed?

Paige rushed into their huge walk-in closet. All of his clothes hung in his usual obsessively neat, color-coordinated rows. She tugged on Antonio's jewelry display drawer. His watch collection (his most prized possession) were all still there. All 30 of them, some with diamonds that sparkled in the light.

Paige's shoulders slumped with relief, but her legs gave out until she slid to the floor with her back against the wall. She pulled her knees up to her chest and rocked. She hadn't felt this scared and anxious since the time she'd found out about Antonio's first marriage misdeed. Paige shivered and swiped her hands over her face. Was this what had caused her to assume the worst this time automatically? Had she been like this for years now? Paige thought she'd gotten over things, but at that moment, she realized she was still shell-shocked. Her life was like one big minefield that she'd been tiptoeing around, hoping nothing else would explode.

Paige swallowed hard, her throat suddenly aching. She didn't want to relive that time. They were in their early twenties. He'd just gotten used to being famous, having money. Women were constantly throwing themselves at him. Paige had found out about one girl. Antonio said she didn't mean anything to him. He had grabbed Paige and held onto her the day she had confronted him, holding the pictures out in front of her with tears running down her cheeks. Paige had forgiven Antonio, and that was that. Wasn't it? She'd told herself for years that she was over it all. That what had happened was the price of fame. They were so young at the time. Antonio had let the money get to his head, but he loved her. That's what he'd said. He loved her, and no one else meant anything to him. Michaela had encouraged Paige to stay. She had championed Antonio's cause. Paige thought strangely about the conversation she'd had with Michaela today. It was always odd how Michaela could be on her side, but on Antonio's side at the same time.

After a few minutes, Paige pulled herself up with every bit of strength she had left, feeling as if she were pulling herself from dangling over the side of a tall building.

"There's a perfect explanation for all of this, I'm sure," she mumbled as she dialed Antonio's number. She had taught herself that everything had a perfect explanation. It was another coping mechanism.

Paige's call went straight to voicemail. She sighed. Another ripple of nervous nausea trampled through her gut. Her hands shook as she redialed her husband's number. The same thing happened. Still, Paige called Antonio's phone over and over. She couldn't help herself. It was the same obsessive behavior she'd exhibited during that time in the past. The pictures of Antonio and that girl had come straight to Paige's private email. How had the girl gotten her email? That was the question Antonio had gotten stuck on back then. Paige had never figured it out, but she'd certainly felt the same as she did now, like her feelings were a beer can being crushed under the giant foot of a drunken biker, reduced to nothing but a flat piece of trash.

When Antonio had returned from the road back then, he'd rushed into the house with tears in his eyes and a huge diamond ring—a peace offering, or now that she thought back, maybe it was a shut-up-and-live-with-it gift. Paige had laid in her bed, sick, for three days after that. Antonio had loved her back to health. He worked hard to regain her trust. Their lovemaking had been more explosive than it had ever been. They fell in love all over again. He'd promised (no, sworn on his mother's grave) that he would never hurt her again.

Paige dialed Antonio again. Still nothing. She went back downstairs and checked their five-car garage, though she knew Antonio wasn't there. She walked the expansive hallway of their home to Antonio's office. She paused at the threshold and inhaled. His MVP trophies, his Olympic medals, pictures of him with past presidents, and plaques of appreciation from his hometown were all displayed like a mini museum. The Museum of Antonio Roberts. Paige rushed over to his desk. With a flourish, she sifted through the stacks of papers on top. Her eyes scanned for any words related to their money. Nothing. She tugged on the tarnished brass handles of the desk drawers. She let out a grunt when she found that the drawers were all locked.

Paige collapsed into Antonio's desk chair. Her head pounded. This feeling of helplessness was familiar, and Paige had always told herself she would not be in this predicament again. But, here she was. She picked up her cell phone and stabbed at the buttons. This time she tried Antonio's best friend, Rich. Nothing. Paige blew out a hard breath. She stormed out of the office and into her kitchen.

"Where are you? What have you done?" She tossed her phone onto her counter and ran her hands through her hair. She needed something to take the edge off, but she didn't drink. Paige yanked open the built-in wine cooler that she usually only opened when she had company. She looked inside and read some of the fancy names on the bottles. She grabbed a bottle of Sweet Walter Red, a cheap, sweet red wine, probably the only wine she could stand to drink since she hated the taste of alcohol. Michaela had chastised Paige for even having the eight-dollar bottle of wine in a wine cooler housed in a mansion kitchen. Paige examined the bottle for a few minutes, thinking. She had better get used to drinking cheap wine, since now she was broke now. *Was* she broke?

With trembling hands, Paige poured a full glass of the deep burgundy wine and took a big gulp. She winced. Even the sweet stuff didn't taste sweet.

Paige wanted to call her mother, but it was late, and her mother would know she was upset. There would be so many questions. Her mother had a keen sixth sense when it came to Paige's drama, but not much else where Paige was concerned. When Paige was younger, being a wife was the only thing her mother expected of her. Her mother would say, "Marriage is a woman's purpose." She fed that into Paige's little head from the time Paige could say the alphabet up to the part where most kids turned the letters into a sing-song that sounded more like *ELA-MEN-OPEE* than *L, M, N, O, P.*

"Paigey," her mother would say. "You're so pretty. Those gray eyes and that long, sandy hair will get you the richest, most handsome husband when the time comes." All through high school, her mother obsessed over who Paige had a crush on and who she dated more than she did. Paige never let her mother know how much anxiety the constant badgering about marriage had brought her. And her mother certainly acted as if she didn't notice the bouts of depression, when Paige would retreat to her wing of their estate for days at a time without eating, bathing, or going to school.

Paige stared into the bottom of her empty glass. She realized that she'd lived her entire life for other people. First her parents, then Michaela, then Antonio, and now Antonio and Christian. She didn't have anything of her own, not even experiences. Everything she'd experienced in life had come from other people. Paige had attended the finest schools, traveled to mystical places around the world at a young age, taken music lessons, dance lessons, starred in debutante balls, and never wanted for anything thanks to her parents. Paige's fun years could be credited to Michaela. Paige would've never snuck out of the house, partied (oh, and did they party), experimented with weed, backpacked around Europe, and had fun, sneaky, exciting sex out of wedlock, if it weren't for Michaela. Even finding the joy in parenthood had been thanks to Antonio. Paige had suffered the worst bout of postpartum depression after Christian was born, but Antonio's constant urging and support helped her get over it. She'd eventually snuggled up to her baby boy, inhaled his scent, and formed a bond with him that she hadn't thought possible. Everything. Everything Paige did in life had depended on other people. Even now, she co-owned everything with Antonio, and she stood to inherit the rest. Nothing was hers and hers alone. Not even her son. The thought of how empty her life was made her take the wine bottle to the head this time.

She thought about her son. Her first son. The one that she had lost in the stress of Antonio's indiscretion. Just like a man, she thought, only thinking about himself. They were so young at the time and unmarried, and the stress of her reputation being at risk, as well as the cheating, almost put her in the hospital. But when Antonio showed how much he loved her, it felt like nothing else mattered, and she recovered. She could remember the day five years ago that she told Antonio she was pregnant. She had bought a pair of baby Air Jordans that matched his favorite pair. When he came home and saw, he almost cried.

From that moment on, Christian was their world, both Paige and Antonio. A perfect reconciliation of their relationship. He looked so much like his daddy that she couldn't look at him and not think of Antonio. With his dark curls and brown skin to match, he seemed to have the best of both of them. He had a laugh that would fill the house, and he was fast, so fast that Antonio wanted to put him on a court already, but she had said no. She thought that one day he would be a tall, gangly sixteen-year-old like Antonio, that then he could follow in his father's footsteps. But for now, he was still her baby, her redemption after the first initial heartbreak she had suffered. Even tonight as he spent the night at Michaela's, she missed him.

"What do you have without him? Who are you without them?" she murmured, speaking to the sketch on the bottle of a woman and little man in a French beret. She took another swig of wine. Her insides warmed up, but she didn't feel better. She was mad at the tears sliding down her face. She'd let this happen. It was her fault.

"You need your own career. Your own money. You need control of your life. Take control of your life. To hell with everyone else." That sounded practical as she said it, but Paige didn't even know where to start. How does one go from being a kept little girl to a kept woman, and suddenly stand on her own? Paige hugged the bottle of wine to her chest, tucked her legs under her, and curled up on the couch in her family room. "That's it, Paige. Take control of your life." The thought, easier said than done, crossed her mind right before she fell into an anxious sleep.

Chapter 3

Living Up To It

Antonio took a deep breath before he turned the door-knob and entered the house through the garage. His legs felt heavy as lead, and his eyes like someone had thrown a handful of sand in his face. He'd prayed all the way home that Paige was upstairs in Christian's bed asleep, which was what she usually did when she was mad at him. It would make things easier for him. He needed a mental break.

Antonio looked down at his watch, and it was 2:30 in the morning. He knew his wife well enough to know that she'd be thinking the worst. For the second time in less than 24 hours, dread loomed over Antonio until he felt like someone had thrown a black bag over his head . . . over his life for that matter.

Antonio crept through the family room, taking care not to make too much noise. In the darkness, he didn't see Paige until she was on him.

"Where have you been? Why did you take all the money? What is wrong with you?" Paige came out, screaming and pounding her fist against his chest.

Antonio stumbled back a few steps. "Wait, Paige. Shh."

Paige swung her arms wildly, and her voice cracked with anguish. "You had me looking like a fool in front of everyone! How could you?"

"Shh." He wrapped her up in a tight bear hug. "Paige, calm down." He struggled with her.

"Get off of me," she yelled through gritted teeth, fighting against his strong grip.

"Calm down. Let me talk to you," he said, feeling her strength waning.

"How could you?" Paige collapsed against his chest, finally worn out. "Why?" she whimpered.

"I know you're upset, but I can explain everything." He held her and guided her over to the couch. He could smell the wine on her breath. He knew she could smell the whiskey on his.

"What did you do?" Paige asked, her voice trembling.

"I thought I was doing the right thing, Paige. I swear I did." He released her and hung his head. "I told you that I made some investments. Well, what I didn't tell you was that they were with Rich."

Paige's head shot up. "What?" Her voice was thin and reedy like a sick person's.

"I know what you're thinking, but I'm telling you, shit was solid. I researched it. I swear I did. It was a hedge fund that had outperformed all others. The money was going into several different businesses. It was a good deal. What I thought was foolproof."

"And?" Paige asked, lowering her face into her hands.

"It fell apart. I put everything into it, and it fell apart."

Paige sucked in her breath and fell against Antonio's shoulder again. He could feel her trembling. He'd lived poor before, but Paige hadn't. His stomach churned. He'd ruined their lives. He hated to disappoint her like this. Again.

"And, I can't find Rich. Whatever was left, he's gone with it." Antonio felt a sharp stab in his chest as he said the words. All the way home, he'd promised to be honest with Paige. No more lies. Not even to protect Rich, like he'd done so many times in the past.

Her shoulders rose and fell with an "it figures" and "I told you so" shrug.

Antonio had been friends with Richard Durn since they were kids. Rich was the person who'd gotten him through his years growing up in the projects without so much as a scratch. Rich would fight all of Antonio's battles. He was of the streets. Everything about the streets was in Rich's blood. He had been there for Antonio through his struggles in life, including the death of his mother. Antonio had always felt an unbreakable sense of loyalty to his best friend and didn't want to admit that he recognized what others had been telling him for years: Rich was trouble. Rich had ridden Antonio's coattails the entire time Antonio played in the NBA. Others, including Paige, would tell Antonio that Rich was an opportunist, but Antonio was blinded by his loyalty to his friend. Even when it was obvious.

Antonio had just wanted to get lunch. Rich, as usual, was late. They weren't at a fancy restaurant, but somehow Rich still managed to be underdressed, in his overly baggy jeans, bedazzled T-shirt, and inexplicable winter coat. Antonio was almost annoyed, but Rich cracked that same smile he always did, and his anger vanished in the nostalgia of their friendship. Rich was more a brother than anything else.

"Sorry, man, I got caught up handling some business," Rich said in the way he always did, where Antonio knew he was lying but preferred not to know anyway. He poured himself some water and drank it all in one gulp.

"No worries, I was just chilling, I don't have shit else going on," Antonio paused, his nerves getting the best of him, "I don't know if you've heard yet—"

Rich cut him off. "I already know. You know I have eyes and ears everywhere," he said while flagging down a waiter and opening a menu, everything one swift motion. He looked at the menu while Antonio sat quietly, angry his friend seemed so nonchalant about his world ending.

"So, you're just not going to—" Antonio started before Rich cut him off again.

"Chill, my guy. I found a way to fix your problem," Rich replied before hearing the question, knowing that he was annoying Antonio by not letting him talk. He smirked. "See, when I heard that you had been dropped, my first instinct was to go fuck up that dumbass manager of yours, since he clearly doesn't know what the fuck he doing, but then I thought, do Antonio even care about ball that much? We getting old."

Antonio scoffed. He knew his body was at this peak, and that his career ending had more to do with the politics of it all and less about his prowess on the court.

"I told you all those years ago that marrying that little daddy's girl was going to come back and bite you in the ass," Rich had to pause to order his food, and Antonio took his chance.

"What the fuck are you talking about, Rich? Just say it," Antonio said before his friend could open his mouth again. This is how things often went between them. Rich knew that he would not be living the life he did without Antonio, but Antonio knew that he would not be living the life that he did without Rich's support throughout their teen years. They were both completely and totally indebted to each other, and for Rich that meant that he could talk to NBA star Antonio Roberts any which way he wanted.

"I have an investment opportunity for you," Rich said, leaning back in his chair and putting his fingers together like some sort of Bond villain. Antonio almost laughed out loud.

"Nah, get out of here, man, you know I don't fuck with that life. Keep it."

"Listen, you trust me, right?" Rich leaned forward in his seat. Who knew Antonio better than he did?

"You know I trust you with my life, but my money is something else," Antonio shifted in his chair. He didn't like thinking that his status had pulled him away from that boy who used to post up in his living room all those years ago.

"Alright, say less, but, at least listen to what I have to say. This isn't just me, this isn't just you, there is a whole mess of other investors moving capital in my direction. Or at least they want to. The money is there and ready, but I'm not Antonio Roberts. People don't trust me the way they trust you." Rich was talking slower and slower, and Antonio could feel where this was going.

"Rich—"

"Listen, if you don't trust me—if you really don't trust me—look at the portfolio for the company," he reached into his puffy jacket and pulled out a slightly bent manila folder that he must have had under his arm the whole time. Antonio was surprised by his friend's preparedness. Usually when he came to ask for money, he only brought his flashy smile and his knowledge of Antonio's guilt for getting out of the hood.

Antonio looked through the documents that Rich laid out on the table. And for the first time began to seriously consider that maybe he was on to something.

"Listen, Paige ain't the one to be broke and struggling, you know that. Your son deserves better than you did, you know that. Make this move, preserve your future."

Antonio was still flipping through papers. He knew from the moment that he met Paige that as much as he loved her or as much as she loved him, nothing compared to the way money ruled their lives. It didn't matter if it was his lack or her surplus. Either way, it was an important part of their relationship. Where else was he supposed to get the money Paige needed to live her life now that the one thing that had him on the come up was gone?

"I'll think about it," Antonio said. Rich smiled.

Paige's voice brought Antonio back.

"Okay, so you invested some and lost it, but you took everything out of the bank and shut down the credit cards. . . . Why?" Paige sat back up, her face stony. She needed answers, he could tell.

Antonio sighed. "I had to, Paige. There were other investors. These people invested in the company just on the strength of me, my name, my star power. But when this happened," he shook his head. "The claws came out. The investors called me to a meeting this morning, and they were demanding their money back. Rumors were flying. They were saying it was all a Ponzi scheme and they were going to take me down. I tried to explain to them that I was in the same position as they were, if not worse." The words fell from Antonio's lips like big, heavy cinder blocks.

"Ponzi scheme?" Paige repeated. Her cheeks were flushed, and her hands shook.

Antonio closed his eyes and cleared his throat to keep it from completely closing on him. He felt like he was telling his wife he'd betrayed her all over again.

"How much did we lose?" Paige asked, sternly.

"Millions."

Just like the people he'd convinced to invest in Rich's business venture, Antonio had lost millions. His last. Their last. Practically everything they had for their future.

"It was my name on their contracts. Rich had drawn up the company's ownership papers and filed the licenses. We were listed as partners on everything, but it wasn't an equal partnership. On paper, I owned 80 percent of the company. I didn't even know it until one of the investors literally threw her contract in my face."

Antonio's head throbbed thinking about it. That same irate investor happened to be the niece of a high-ranking federal agent. She had let Antonio know that if he didn't return her money immediately, she and all the investors would be going to her uncle's office before the end of the day. He'd be in trouble with the Feds, on top of losing everything.

"That's why I had to gather up all the cash that I could, including the cash advances on the cards. I had to save my ass, Paige. I'm in way deep."

"So, we're broke, and you're in legal trouble?" Paige asked, her eyes stretched in disbelief.

"I'm going to fix it."

"Oh my God," Paige gasped.

"Look, I have enough cash on hand to take care of the bills for a couple of months until I can make the money back. We'll have to cut back on the extra stuff."

"But how, Antonio?"

"Don't worry. I will take care of it. I always do," he said, putting his arm around her and pulling her closer to him. Paige was stiff against him, her anger, fear, and disappointment like a force field between them.

"Trust me." He stroked her hair. "I'm not going to let anything happen to us." He kissed the top of her head. He moved slightly so that she would have to face him.

"I love you." He gently ran his thumb down her cheeks to wipe away her tears. "Do you hear me? I would never let you go without."

Paige closed her eyes. Some of the tension in her features eased. She looked like a wounded soldier surrendering.

Antonio leaned in and kissed her.

Although her body was tense, Antonio knew how to set things straight between them. It had worked so many times in the past.

"I'm sorry," he murmured as he ran his hands up her shirt.

"Me too," Paige sighed. She didn't fight him away.

"Just give me a chance to fix it," Antonio whispered, pulling her shirt over her head.

Paige made a mousy noise as Antonio moved lower and tugged her pants over her hips, then past her ankles.

Antonio felt at ease now. This was their normal. Fight, fuck, fix things. It had been going on since they were teenagers.

"I'm going to take care of you." He lowered his mouth to hers again. Paige leaned up and kissed him back, first slowly and then more passionately. Antonio felt Paige's heart against his chest. He still had it. She still loved him. He moved his mouth to her neck, then trailed his tongue down the center of her chest, over her belly button, and finally, he dropped to his knees between her legs.

Paige let out an audible breath when he moved his tongue to her inner thighs. He kissed the insides of each thigh gently. Paige trembled.

"Oh my God, I love you," Paige huffed, her voice gruff with lust. That was what Antonio needed to hear. He needed reassurance that he'd won her over again. That he was living up to her standards again.

Paige panted through her slightly opened lips, letting out a small gasp. "Yes," she whispered lustfully, lifting her hips slightly toward Antonio's mouth.

He thrust his long, wet tongue deeper. He used his hands to gently part her. He tasted her. He drank her up. He let their problems fall out of his mind.

"I need you," Paige begged. "All of you." Antonio could tell she was crying. This was a scene he'd certainly lived before. Tears of joy, pain, hurt, and satisfaction all together.

Antonio stood up and pulled her until her hips were hanging off the edge of the couch.

"Ah," Paige winced, squeezing her eyes shut as Antonio filled her up. She lifted her pelvis in response to his rhythmic thrusts. Their bodies moved in sync.

"Oh, God!" Paige belted out. Her inner thighs vibrated from the explosion of pleasure filling her body. Her screams urged Antonio on. He moved faster, grinding into her pelvis with longer, deeper strokes. Her slippery walls responded immediately, pulsating and squeezing him tight. He pounded their problems away. This was their love language.

"Ah!" Paige screamed out, tightening her legs around his waist as her walls pulsed in and out. Antonio followed with a muscle-tensing climax of his own. He collapsed on Paige's chest. She reached down and stroked his head gently.

"I'm sorry all of this is happening," he said, the first to speak.

"I should've been more understanding. You were right. It's not all about material things," Paige said regretfully. There was a short pause.

"I'm going to ask my father for a job," she said.

Antonio lifted his head, tilting it slightly, waiting for her to explain.

"I think it's time that I contribute," Paige explained. "I need something of my own too."

Antonio sat up. "I didn't mean that the other day. I told you when we got married that I would take care of you, and I will."

Damn, he thought the good sex was going to do what it usually did—squash the argument.

"I just think it's time that I take charge of my own life, Antonio. Everything you pointed out the other night . . . the things you referred to as extra, is my lifestyle, what I've been accustomed too. I'm going to go talk to my father, because he can pull some strings and put me in a position where I can earn some money, right away. I mean, I do have my degree. Why not use it?"

Antonio's jaw rocked feverishly. "You're not going to your father. Matter of fact, you better not say a word to him. I won't have him looking at me like I failed you . . . again. I'm tired of trying to live up, Paige. Let me handle this. I already have a meeting set up with Emil Cartwright. I'm the one who will be getting a job . . . not you."

Paige stood up. "Emil Cartwright? *The* Emil Cartwright? You can't be serious, Antonio." She snatched up her clothes and thrust her legs into her pants.

"Look, don't be judgmental," Antonio said, knowing exactly where she was going with the conversation.

"He's a criminal for God's sake," Paige countered. "My father is a senator. His son-in-law can't be associated with the Cartwrights. My family name can't be tarnished by that association. Besides, I never told my parents about—"

Antonio put his hand up, halting her words. "Let's not talk about the difference between alleged criminals and politicians, Paige. Emil has never been convicted of any crimes. There seem to be a bunch of people hell-bent on keeping him down, but he rises above it every time. It's pretty fascinating if you ask me. Cartwright Enterprises is legitimate, with earnings in the hundreds of millions," Antonio said, defensive.

"And how has that served you all of these years?" Paige retorted.

Antonio squinted. Her words were a low blow. "It hasn't, but that's because I didn't allow it to. But, right now, I think it's as good a time as any to collect on what is owed to me."

Paige seemed to contemplate this. Antonio stretched his arms over his head. "Look, you worry too much. This is all going to work out. Let's go to bed. Long day ahead of me tomorrow." The discussion was over. He needed to be sharp for his meeting. It had the potential to change his life—*their* lives. Forever.

The next day Antonio's leg felt weak as he walked into the shiny, glass front building on Wall Street, down in Manhattan's Financial District. He'd heard that Emil Cartwright had purchased the building a year ago for 38 million dollars. Cash.

Antonio exhaled as he looked up at the huge, mirrored gold letters that read: CARTWRIGHT ENTERPRISES. He wondered what it would be like to be part of a family like the Cartwrights, who had their name on properties all over the city where he'd grown up. Sure, Antonio was famous, but this was different. The Cartwrights had generational wealth, a legacy. Their name rang bells (some good, some bad), not just in New York, but all over the nation.

"Can I help you, sir?" a pretty, raven-haired receptionist greeted him.

A wave of nausea crashed through Antonio's stomach. Antonio couldn't figure out if it were excitement or fear or both. It had taken a lot for him to swallow his pride and ask Emil for this meeting. He didn't know whether it was even considered a meeting when you shared the same blood.

"I have an appointment with Mr. Cartwright."

The receptionist smiled like she wanted to laugh at him, "Which Mr. Cartwright, sir?"

Antonio's brows knitted slightly. His cheeks warmed up.

"The father or the sons?" the receptionist clarified, noticing the confusion on Antonio's face.

The heat moved to his belly. "Oh, I just assumed . . . um . . . sorry. . . . Emil Cartwright. The father." My father.

Antonio's heart hammered now. The word "sons" had thrown him off. He had to pull it together. Of course, Emil Cartwright had sons. Antonio had known this for years. He also knew they'd had the privilege of growing up with their father and his wealth.

Antonio followed the receptionist into a huge conference room with a wall of windows that looked out at the water and skyline. The room smelled like brand new furniture and everything inside was modern and shiny. The long, mahogany table was surrounded by at least twenty plush leather rolling office chairs. This must be the place Emil Cartwright conducted all his important business meetings. Antonio suddenly felt important. He tugged on his suit jacket lapels and adjusted his tie.

"There's water in the bucket here, a few snacks, and here is the remote for the television," the receptionist said, pointing out everything. "It'll just be a few more minutes. Mr. E is finishing up another meeting."

This felt like an official business meeting, on the one hand, then on the other, Antonio felt like a lost boy. Antonio nodded at the receptionist. He still hadn't found his voice. In fact, being there made him feel awkward, like how he imagined a kid meeting his adoptive family for the first time would feel—excited, apprehensive, and scared shitless all at the same time.

Antonio walked over to the wall of windows and stared out at the place he'd grown up. There were so many questions swirling in his head. Why had he and his mother been left to live in the worst projects in the Bronx? Growing up, even when his mother smiled, Antonio had always sensed that she lived with a deep sadness she just couldn't shake. Antonio hadn't asked his questions the first time he'd met Emil Cartwright because he had been overwhelmed with too many emotions.

Suddenly, a memory emerged in Antonio's mind as clear as an REM-sleep dream. Antonio had held his mother's frail hand in his as the monitors next to her bed blipped a song. A final, sad song. He'd felt a crushing sensation in his chest when the doctors had told him those were her last days. Sclerosis of the liver, they'd said. Antonio didn't even know what that meant. He had said all he could say and had prayed in earnest as much as he could. Still, nothing had changed. He was losing her.

Antonio had his head down on her bed when he heard the footsteps to his left. He hadn't bothered to lift his head. He figured it was another doctor coming with more bad news.

"Cynthia?" A deep voice had croaked out, the syllables rising and falling with emotion.

Antonio lifted his head at the sound of his mother's name. But, it wasn't just the name, it was the shakiness in the voice. He stared at the well-dressed man standing at the foot of his mother's bed. The man acted as if Antonio was invisible as he walked to the other side of the bed and picked up Antonio's mother's hand. Antonio had sprung to his feet, his jaw set tight.

"Cynthia, my one true love," the man rasped, raw emotion evident behind his words. "I'm sorry. I'm so sorry."

"Who are you?" Antonio growled, squaring off, his mother's body the line in the sand.

"Um, well . . ." the stranger started, but before the man or Antonio could speak again, his mother's voice caused both of their heads to turn.

"Ma," Antonio huffed. Tears of joy immediately welled up in his eyes.

"Emil," his mother finally managed, moving her head slowly in the direction of the man.

Antonio's brow creased, and his mouth hung slightly open as he watched the exchange. The man, a big, strong, strapping man, seemed to be reduced to a shell of grief. His shoulders rocked, and he let out audible sobs.

Antonio watched, confused. If his mother hadn't been so sick, he would've demanded that the stranger identify himself or leave. But, something in her eyes had told Antonio that she was happy to see this man.

"Ma," Antonio said just above a whisper.

His mother turned her head toward him.

"Baby, this . . ." She started coughing violently. The monitors rang loudly.

Alarmed, Antonio squeezed her hand. He didn't like to see her in this kind of pain. "Shh, Ma. . . . Don't try to talk."

She shook her head adamantly. She opened her mouth again but still couldn't get the words out. Whatever she had to say, it was important.

Antonio held one hand, the stranger held her other hand.

"This is . . . your. . ." his mother wheezed, trying to get the words out.

"Antonio. I'm sorry for the delay," Emil Cartwright called out as he whisked into the Cartwright Enterprises conference room.

Startled out of his thoughts, Antonio spun around to face him. Antonio blinked a few times, struck by the feeling that he was looking into a time elapsed mirror.

Emil hadn't changed much since Antonio's last encounter with him. The noticeable speckles of gray hair that sat in a neat patch on the top of Emil's head and his almost completely silver mustache were the only big changes. Those were also the only signs that he'd aged. Emil stood over six feet tall, and his slender frame showed no signs of the pudginess some older men developed as they aged. He was still as regal as he was the times Antonio had seen him in the past. But now, with everything he'd learned about the man over the years, Antonio recognized the significance of Emil's custom-tailored Armani suits, monogrammed solid gold cufflinks, and diamond-encrusted watch.

Antonio's eyes glinted with recognition. He touched the cleft in his chin, a subliminal message, a display of comfort and ease around his son.

"No worries," Antonio said, extending his hand for a shake. "I'm sorry, myself, for this last-minute request to meet."

"You make it sound so formal," Emil said, pulling Antonio into him for a quick brother-man hug—a shoulder-to-shoulder tap and pat on the back.

Antonio was a bit thrown off by the show of affection.

"Please, have a seat," Emil said, pulling out the chair at the head of the conference table.

Antonio put his hands up in front of him. "I can sit anywhere. Really." He didn't feel like he belonged at the head of that important table.

"Nonsense. Sit. Sit. Make yourself comfortable," Emil urged. He pulled out a side chair for himself.

Antonio squeezed his hands shut to keep them from shaking. As a kid growing up without a father, Antonio would imagine that his father was a strong man with huge hands and feet that could beat the world. He would walk down the street and stare at men, wondering if any of them were his father. When he'd ask his mother, she'd always say he didn't need a father because Antonio was just a gift to her from someone who loved her very much. Antonio had always assumed she meant God, and now, staring at a silver-haired, boldly confident and wealthy Emil Cartwright, maybe his assumption was right.

"Well, I won't take up a lot of your time," Antonio said, leaning forward on his arms. "I don't want you to think I'm here because, well, you know. . . ."

Emil put his hand up. "It's been years. If you were that person, you would've done that years ago."

Some of the tension in Antonio's shoulders eased. The last thing he wanted was to come across like he needed a handout or was begging for reparations for how he'd grown up.

"I just need a job. Things took a turn—"

"You know, for years, I wanted to be around you," Emil blurted.

Antonio's mouth snapped shut. He swallowed hard, trying to get rid of the hard lump that had formed in his throat.

"Things were complicated with your mother and me. But, she was the only woman I ever really loved. That's the honest truth," Emil said, lowering his eyes like he could no longer look in Antonio's.

Antonio didn't know what to say. He wanted to know the story, but he hadn't found the courage to ask.

"I was married. She was engaged to someone else. We fell in love. Real love. We both realized that if we chose to be together, things would get messy. I swear I didn't know she had gotten pregnant. I swear it," Emil said with sincerity. He looked at Antonio seriously, "I would've never left any son of mine behind like that. I didn't know until that day I saw you. I'd kept up with Cynthia over the years, but she always managed to keep me from seeing you. I knew she had broken off her engagement and lived her life alone with you. For some years, she shut me out. She forced me to stay in my marriage. I would have left everything behind for her. I swear it. Your mother was the only woman I ever really loved."

"She was sad about it," Antonio said barely above a whisper. He felt his tear ducts about to betray him, but he fought them back.

Emil moved to the edge of his seat and stared at Antonio.

"When I got old enough to understand, I figured out why she drank so much. Why she moved to the drugs. She would drown her sorrows in drugs and alcohol, sometimes cry through the night, but she would always be up the next day to make sure I had what I needed. She came to all of my games. I smelled the alcohol on her, I saw her losing weight by the tens, but I was never embarrassed by her. I knew there was some great pain she was struggling with. I just didn't know what. She was my best friend. She was everything to me. I didn't know it was you that had hurt her like that," Antonio said, tears rimming his eyes now. He refused to let them fall.

Emil opened his mouth to apologize, but he never got the chance.

"Pop, sorry we're late."

Emil startled and turned around in his chair. Antonio looked over Emil's shoulder as two men rushed into the conference room. Antonio sat up straighter, quickly swiping at his face to make sure it wasn't wet. He remembered them—Hayden and Jackson Cartwright. They'd been there with Emil the first time Emil had mustered up the courage to approach Antonio after his mother had died.

"Have a seat," Emil pointed across the table.

Hayden, dressed in a tailored suit like his father, obeyed his father's instruction without question.

"What? We're supposed to take a side seat while this dude sits at the head?" Jackson spat, glaring at Antonio from under his New York Yankees fitted cap. He stood in stark contrast to his well-dressed brother.

Antonio tightened his jaw, but he didn't speak. Instead, his eyes darted to Emil.

"Jax, sit down," Emil said, sternly this time. It was an order, not an invitation.

Jackson sighed loudly and yanked one of the rolling chairs away from the conference table.

"You both remember Antonio," Emil said, a hint of discomfort in his tone.

Antonio could tell it was itching Emil to say, "My son and your brother, Antonio."

"Yeah, you should remember him too. The dude just embarrassed your ass in front of thousands of people," Jackson shot back.

Antonio could tell right away Jackson was the loose cannon of the family. He even dressed contrary to his father and brother with his low-hung designer jeans, thick Cuban link chain lying on a plain black t-shirt, fitted cap, and brand new crisp white designer sneakers. If clothes depicted night and day, in Antonio's assessment, Hayden would've been day and Jackson would've been night.

"That's the past," Hayden interjected. "I remember him. Of course." He looked directly at Antonio. "In fact, I've followed your career. When our mother passed away, and Pop told us about you, I wasn't angry at him. I was confused about why he'd let things go the way they did. If I had it my way, you would've been around before now. It must've been tough growing up the way you did and then finding out things could've been much different for you."

Antonio nodded. "Appreciate it." But, he didn't. A fire lit in his belly. He felt like some strange interloper who was fascinating for them to watch. Someone to pity. Hayden's statement made Antonio feel more like a charity case than before. Still, Antonio played it off.

"I'm bringing Antonio into the fold here at C.E.," Emil announced proudly like he'd just recruited Antonio from a pile of highly touted applicants. "He will work hand-in-hand with both of you until he learns the ropes. He will be on equal footing. He'll learn everything there is to know." Emil looked from Jackson to Hayden, and then to Antonio. "Everything," he stressed.

Jackson laughed sinisterly. "You can't be serious, Pop. You just trust this dude off the rip? No questions asked? All of a sudden he's your son and our equal? Why is he coming around now? What changed for him? Who sent him? Ain't like he gave you a big fatherly hug when you tried in the past. I don't trust this nigga."

Emil, Antonio, and Hayden all shifted uncomfortably in their seats. Jackson was right. Antonio had wanted nothing to do with Emil before now. They all recalled the year Emil had bought courtside tickets to Antonio's game and he'd taken Jackson and Hayden along. Emil had beamed proudly as he watched his other son play up close for the first time. When Antonio had noticed Emil sitting courtside at his NBA game, he played his ass off. He'd hit his first triple-double of the season. After the game, Emil used his powerful connections to get onto the court. He'd walked up to Antonio with a proud grin spread across his face.

"Antonio," Emil had called out, his hand ready for a shake.

Antonio had shot him a dirty look. "No autographs today. I don't do deadbeats," he'd grumbled and pushed past him.

Apparently, Jackson still held that grudge.

"That was the past. It was complicated. We've worked it out," Emil said, smiling over at Antonio now.

We did? Antonio wondered. He returned a halfhearted smile. He needed this, so whatever hesitancy he was feeling toward Emil, he swallowed it whole. It had no place right now. He'd kept up with Emil over the years. He had done some digging after Emil's first big trial hit the media. The Feds had thrown all sorts of charges at Emil, including murder and racketeering. Back then, Antonio had become obsessed with the story. He'd watched Emil masterfully turn the Feds' case on its ear. Antonio had wanted to stay angry at Emil for abandoning him as a child, but somewhere deep inside he was proud of the man. He was proud he had his blood running through his veins.

"I'm excited to have you on board." Hayden stood and extended his hand toward Antonio. "Whatever Pop wants, I'll accommodate."

Antonio shook Hayden's hand. "I appreciate it."

Emil watched them, satisfaction easing across his features. His expression quickly changed at the sound of Jackson's chair hitting the wall when he shot up out of it in a fury.

"You're making a mistake. All of a sudden he's your son? This dude thought he was too good when he played in the League. He married into that stuck-up-ass Tillary family, and he couldn't see himself as your son all these years. So, what changed? He's working with his father-in-law? That nigga been after you for years!"

They all sat, riveted by Jackson's angry outburst. Emil was embarrassed, Hayden was slightly amused, and Antonio felt exposed, like he'd been stripped naked in front of a crowd.

Jackson turned his heated gaze toward Antonio. "My father might trust you, but I don't. I'm the eldest Cartwright heir, I don't give a fuck what year a whore laid down with my father and decided to—"

Antonio shot up from his chair, his fists balled.

Emil stepped in front of Jackson. "That's enough. He's my son, he's a part of this family, he's entitled to what I say he's entitled to, and he works for me now. Just like you. End of discussion."

Antonio and Jackson's eyes locked. They were more alike than they knew.

Chapter 4

Faking It

Paige rushed through the huge cherry wood French doors of the Riverdale Country Club. With more faking it to come, her head throbbed. She was late, and she knew how her mother hated her to be late.

Once inside, Paige's stomach clenched at the sight of all of the extremely rich women milling about in their big hats, sparkly and gaudy estate jewelry, and custom-made dresses and Chanel suits. Paige wanted to vomit. This was real wealth. Old money. This definitely wasn't rich-because-your-husband-played-sports money or a rich-because-your-mother-married-up type of wealth.

"Ah, Ms. Tillary, we were expecting you," a tall blonde with a clipboard chimed as soon as Paige approached.

"Roberts," Paige corrected like she always did. It was like these people only acknowledged that she was the daughter of Gladstone and Lillian Tillary, and not the wife of Antonio Roberts. It was their way of subtly saying they didn't accept Antonio's type of money, what they called "new money."

"Right! Forgive me . . . Mrs. Roberts. Either way, we were expecting you," the woman feebly corrected.

Paige smiled weakly. She knew by "expecting you" the woman meant expecting her large monetary contribution. Paige still couldn't say what exactly they did with all those hefty checks they collected every year in the name of charity.

"Has my mother already arrived?" Paige asked, finished with the fake small talk.

"Of course," the blonde chimed. "Your mother is such a gem."

Paige grunted. *You mean such a big money contributor.*

As soon as Paige stepped into the elegantly decorated room, she saw her mother Lillian waving her over to their table. Before now, Paige hadn't thought anything of the fact that she'd paid $500 for one ticket to the country club's annual charity tea. But now, that money seemed like a million dollars to her.

"Paigey! You look radiant," Lillian sang, leaning forward for air kisses on each of Paige's cheeks.

"You look beautiful too, Mom." She meant it too. Lillian Tillary, at age sixty-two, was still a stunner. She kept her body in shape, and her face didn't look older than fifty.

Lillian was a New York City native and the youngest daughter of the wealthy Collette family. Paige had learned early on that her mother had grown up wanting for nothing, even back in the days when black people weren't expected to have the finer things in life. The one thing Lillian did endure was prejudice inside of her own family. The Collettes were very fair-skinned blacks with wavy hair, and they only married people with the same attributes in order to keep the bloodline pure. Lillian, although light skinned, was not as light as her siblings. Her skin was golden and not as pale, and because of her skin tone, she was often treated differently than her siblings. Lillian's grandmother even accused her daughter, Paige's grandmother, of having an affair with a dark-skinned man, and said Lillian was the product of the affair. As with every family, wealthy and poor, the Collette's had their fair share of secrets and crimes too.

Paige fought hard to plaster on a smile as her mother gushed about the same things she always gushed about: who wore what designer, how much so-and-so contributed this year, who was remarrying, and, of course, how great she was doing in all of this.

Faking it was going to be an art in that moment, and Paige needed to master it. She wondered if her mother could see the distress in her eyes or the sadness dragging down the sides of her face as she pretended that she wasn't worried as hell about her life.

"Sit. Sit," Lillian said, pulling out Paige's chair. Paige sat, feeling like she was already on the hot seat. She immediately wished she had made an excuse not to come.

"This year we stand to raise over four hundred thousand more than last year," Lillian said excitedly, clasping her hands together. "I know you're going to bless me with a great contribution, which will just take the totals from my benefactors over the top. I am going to be the highest ranked contributor in our town. I've been fighting for years to surpass that damn Cora Pierre," Lillian continued. These were other bad habits her mother possessed that Paige knew came from her upbringing: competitiveness and jealousy. Lillian hated for anyone, woman or man, to have more or be more than she was in their vast socialite circle. Lillian actually drove Paige crazy with the constant competition.

Paige picked up the champagne flute sitting in front of her all-crystal place setting. To hell with the tea. Paige needed something much stronger to get through the day. She'd found herself drinking more and more these days.

"So, what's it going to be this year, sweet daughter?" Lillian chirped, smiling, the light glinting off of her bright white, perfect veneers. She didn't waste any time getting down to it.

Paige sighed and drained her glass. "Mother, I forgot my checkbook and didn't realize until I was in the car," Paige lied. "I will make it up to you. I promise." She reached over and picked up another champagne flute that obviously wasn't meant for her.

Lillian's smile faded into a scowl. She raised an eyebrow and leaned closer to Paige. "What?" she whispered harshly, her eyes darting around to make sure none of the other pretentious women at their table could hear. "Are you saying you came without a check, Paige?" Lillian's voice was more forceful this time. It reminded Paige of times in her childhood when her mother made her feel like she wasn't good enough, pretty enough, just not enough.

Paige let out a nervous squeak and then cleared her throat, her telltale sign of guilt since she was a child. Lillian grabbed Paige's arm and tugged. She whipped her head around and smiled at other bourgeoisie ladies sitting with them, then turned her attention back to Paige. "Paigey, why don't you walk with me to the loo. I need to freshen up in the powder room," Lillian said, loud enough for the table to hear. She then chuckled nervously as she gripped Paige's arm so tight it started throbbing.

Paige stood up reluctantly as her mother practically dragged her from the table to convene in the restroom. Paige felt like a child all over again. Her mother had often made her feel like she wasn't good enough or like she was a disappointment. When Paige decided to marry Antonio, who her parents thought was beneath her, Lillian stopped speaking to Paige for two months. Paige knew how important appearances were to her mother, but, she'd fallen in love with Antonio, and she wouldn't compromise her own feelings. Not even for her parents.

***

The night that she and Antonio first met, they knew that they had found something special. Even though they were in the middle of a party, Antonio and Paige only had eyes for each other. Her small hand in his big one, they had danced that first song while Rich distracted Michaela with small talk she wasn't interested in.

"So," Rich started, "y'all aren't from around here, are you?" He, unlike Antonio, didn't care about the feelings of rich girls slumming it.

"Obviously not," said Michaela, looking at her delicately manicured nails and thinking about how she loved Paige enough to talk to this lame ass boy so that her friend could be happy. But she had been so sure Antonio was looking at her.

Paige felt butterflies in her stomach the whole time she and Antonio swayed back and forth. She was so distracted by how tall he was and how small she felt in his arms she couldn't even hear the song that was playing, but she trusted him to keep her on the beat. She knew she was safe and protected. Even though she had first thought that the area was dangerous, which it probably was, she felt that with Antonio around, nothing bad would ever happen to her. He looked down at her and tilted his head like he had asked her a question and was waiting for an answer.

"I want to know everything about Paige," he said. And he smiled.

They talked about where they went to school, both slightly embarrassed to admit it to the other. But it was something that could not be avoided.

"Well," began Paige, "my name is Paige Tillary—" She stopped as she felt Antonio's body tense up around her. She almost stumbled on her pumps.

Paige was an illustrious and rich socialite, and Antonio, well, wasn't. Antonio was waiting for his big break, but as he told Paige, that break wasn't too far away. He had been training and playing, and recruiters had been calling him. He knew that he was going to do something. But Antonio knew that name. Everyone knew Gladstone Tillary.

"You mean like, Senator Tillary?" asked Antonio. Paige hated that question.

"Yes," she said. Ever since she was old enough to understand what people were really asking when they brought up her father, she had hated having to explain herself.

"Cool," Antonio responded, "I've never really been into politics, but that must be a fun job." He felt dumb. He didn't know what he was saying. Paige moved closer to him, just missing his instep with her small feet. It wouldn't have hurt him anyway.

She was surprised. Pleased even. Antonio, for all intents and purposes, had gotten his answer and let it go. Most people lingered with it, asking dumb and frustrating questions about what it must be like to have grown up in a house based on appearances how she did, or who her parents had to pay off so that she could have a spot at Riverdale. It was enough to have low self-esteem, another to have it based entirely on someone else. But for the first time, in Antonio, she had found someone who didn't seem to care. Or so she thought.

"Come on," interrupted Rich, leaving Michaela by herself still looking at her nails. "We gotta go," he said, pulling Antonio away from Paige. It seemed that maybe Rich was the one who was really calling the shots.

"Hold up," Antonio said, pulling a pen out of his pocket. Paige smiled. She had never been as bold as she was about to be. She grabbed the pen out of his hand.

"Call me," Paige sang while writing her number across his arm. Antonio looked stunned, like she had just punched him in the stomach. She thought it was cute and dorky, and it only endeared him to her more.

"I will," he winked.

The door slammed, and inside the fancy bathroom, Lillian smiled at a few wrinkled, rich women and waited for them to leave. She turned on Paige so fast her head could've snapped from her neck.

"What is going on, Paige?" Lillian asked, almost through her teeth.

"I told you," Paige fidgeted as sweat made her underarms itch.

"You told me a pack of lies. That's what you told me. Now out with it. Nothing less than the truth." Lillian folded her arms across her chest and tapped her left foot against the floor tiles.

Paige's shoulders slumped, and she sidestepped so she didn't have to look her mother in the eyes. She kicked off her heels, closed her eyes, and sighed loudly. She was always bad at lying, much less holding up under her mother's scrutiny.

"Well?" Lillian pressed. "I am listening."

"Ugh! Mother! Why do you have to know everything? This is the first year I didn't contribute since I've been married and out on my own. Is it such a crime? I forgot my checkbook. Sheesh! Will you die if your daughter doesn't come with a check for this bullshit?" Paige raised her voice, and it shook as she spoke. Her little outburst did not faze her mother one bit.

"Don't try to deflect this onto me, Paige. The first year you're not contributing is a problem. I know you better than—"

"Just stop. I know," Paige interjected rudely. "Yeah, yeah. I've heard it all before." She shook her head in disgust. "That's everyone's problem. Everyone knows Paige better than Paige. Well, think again! No one knows me!"

"What is this all about, Paige?" Lillian softened her voice. "I won't give up until you tell me what's going on." Lillian dropped her arms in an attempt to show she was being more supportive. It worked to ease Paige's anxiety.

"Antonio—"

"I knew it," Lillian jumped in. She couldn't help it. She blamed Antonio for anything that went wrong in Paige's life.

"Let me finish!" Paige snapped. "Geez. You don't know everything. Damn."

Lillian's eyes went wide, but her lips closed. Paige started speaking. As she listened, Lillian squeezed her eyes shut and let out a few gasps as Paige filled her in about her and Antonio's financial crisis.

"And just why the hell didn't you come to us?"

"Because, mother . . . for once, I want to let my husband take care of his family without handouts."

Paige couldn't look her mother in the eyes, so she stared down at her toes.

"I will not have my grandson on the verge of homelessness. What will everyone think if they find out you're broke? Paige, this is unacceptable. You'll be in a shelter. You'll have to beg on the streets. . . ."

"Oh my God, you're so dramatic," Paige replied, shaking her head. "Our broke is not the same as being impoverished, and you know it. We will work it out." Even Paige didn't believe that when she said it.

Lillian giggled, trying to lighten the mood. "What do you need? I can try to help."

"No. I don't want your money and you *ab-so-lutely* cannot, I repeat, *cannot* tell Daddy."

Lillian seemed to contemplate Paige's request. "Well, what's the compromise, Paige? I'll not have you out here hungry and destitute. I cannot afford for the elites to find out you're broke. Not my daughter."

"Will you stop making it seem like we are about to be sleeping on a corner with a cardboard sign and cup, please?"

"I won't tell your father *if* you agree to go to your grandmother and get a loan. I probably can't pull out anything outside of my monthly allowance these days, but your grandmother will help you. You know how she feels about you . . . her little light bright child, as she calls you."

Paige rolled her eyes. She knew her mother wouldn't tell her father, but she also knew if she didn't do what Lillian said and go to her grandmother for some emergency money, Lillian would drive her completely crazy until she did.

"Okay. I will."

"Good," Lillian said, letting out a relieved breath. "But you're not off the hook. Didn't I teach you anything growing up?"

Paige rolled her eyes. She knew what was coming. "What now?"

"Uh . . . stash account? Didn't I teach you that a woman, especially a kept woman, always needs to have her own secret bank account for this same reason? I thought I preached this so much you could recite the exact words in your sleep, Paige. It's called rainy day money . . . get mad money . . . get out money . . . whatever you want to call it, it is important, Paige. I don't want you to struggle. Ever," Lillian said, getting slightly choked up.

Paige knew that her mother's background was the reason she had hammered home these lessons. Although Lillian had grown up wealthy, when her father committed suicide, the following revelation of bad investments and mounds of debt had left Lillian's mother in dire financial straits. One of her father's life insurance policies had lapsed, and the one policy that was good had a limited amount of cash back and was nothing compared to the wealth they were used to. This left Lillian's mother devastated and off to find another wealthy husband. But, when Lillian caught the eye of Gladstone Tillary, of the well-to-do Tillary family, Lillian's mother aggressively encouraged her to accept a date invitation from the future senator.

Lillian thought that the Tillary heir was extremely good looking but too old for her. Feelings aside, Lillian let Gladstone pursue her, and she entertained him. Lillian would've done anything to be in her mother's good graces, knowing and lamenting over the fact that she was her least favorite because of her complexion. Lillian went on that date, and it didn't take long for Gladstone to sweep her off of her feet. After they married, she gave birth to Paige. Paige, with her fair skin, gray eyes, and natural blond hair, was the apple of Lillian's mother's eye. She would do anything for Paige. Anything accept treat Lillian with dignity and love.

"So, the story will be that you're feeling sick . . . maybe even pregnant . . . and had to leave," Lillian whispered. "I don't need these old bags knowing that you didn't contribute. In fact, I'll write a check and pretend it was from you."

Paige sucked her teeth and shook her head. "Okay, mother. I guess we're just going to continue faking it through life, huh?"

"Paige, life is a series of fake-it-til-you-make-it episodes. You should know this by now. Your husband is the pro."

"Goodbye, mother," Paige groaned, hitting the bathroom doors so hard that her palms stung.

Chapter 5

In the Trenches

Antonio had been shown all of Emil's legal business operations: the imported cars, the shipment company, and the overseas markets, but he had yet to be introduced to the part of the business that could make him the fast cash he needed. Antonio had heard that his father made mounds of cash in the streets, but Hayden had been taking baby steps showing him the ropes. Antonio had spent his days and nights learning from Hayden—his smooth, well-dressed, lady-catching brother.

"So, Pop wanted me to talk to you about something," Hayden said, breaking the silence inside of his Mercedes S500.

Antonio looked over at him. "Yeah, whatever you need to say. I'm all ears."

"In order for you to move to the next step in this thing . . . there was something Pop wanted," Hayden said, apprehension in his voice.

"Anything. I already told all of y'all that I'm all about the family."

"That nigga that took you for your paper. Your so-called friend—" Hayden started.

"Rich?"

"Yeah, that rotten-ass nigga. He needs to be dealt with."

Antonio raised his eyebrows. "Dealt with? I don't even know where he ran off to. But, that's him. Over the years, we fall out, and he comes back. He usually makes it good," Antonio said assuredly. "He's basically harmless."

"Nah. That's the point. We need proof you're down for the other side of this business. He has to be taken care of."

Antonio swallowed hard. "Taken care of?"

"Exactly. Taken care of. We are Cartwrights, and we don't let no fuck niggas cross us and get away with it. Pop wants that message sent loud and clear."

Antonio had never heard Hayden speak like this. He was used to the street persona from Jackson, but this was the first time Hayden had showed anything but his refined businessman side. Antonio knew he couldn't back down. His family depended on him.

"Yeah, aight. It's whatever."

"Good. So, let's go," Hayden said, whipping his car around and making such a reckless U-turn that Antonio had to brace himself.

Antonio reluctantly followed Hayden through a maze of doors inside of the nondescript, pale brick building they'd pulled into. He didn't want to seem like a scared bitch, so he hadn't asked any questions, although his shaky legs and pounding heart threatened to betray him. To say Antonio felt faint was an understatement. The sound of his and Hayden's hard-bottom dress shoes ringing off against the laid concrete floors did nothing to ease Antonio's nerves. Finally, they approached a door, and Antonio froze. The familiar voice had stopped him as if he had a pause button on his back.

"Yo! I don't know you niggas! I ain't do shit to you motherfuckers!" Rich barked.

Hayden nodded at Antonio and let him enter the room first. Antonio moved like his feet had suddenly turned into cinder blocks.

"Tony! Yo! What the fuck, man?" Rich screamed, fighting against the heavy nautical rope that bound him to the cold steel chair. "Help me, man! Who the fuck are these people? What the—" Rich screamed, his face turning dark red with a mixture of rage and terror. A crushing blow to his face shut him up for a few seconds. Blood mixed with snot and tears made a mess all over his face. His legs trembled, and his teeth chattered.

Antonio flinched, and his eyes went wide. He blinked rapidly as Jackson came into focus.

"This yo' nigga, right?" Jackson growled. He lodged another balled-fist blow to the left side of Rich's face.

Antonio balled his toes in his shoes, trying his best not to show his discomfort.

"You ready to be a part of this family for real, for real, nigga?" Jackson gritted, getting in Antonio's face.

"C'mon man, just tell—tell me . . . wha . . . what this is about. Tony . . . help me," Rich stuttered, raspy.

"Hah, nigga! God can't even help you right now. Traitor-ass nigga," Jackson chortled as he circled Rich like a flock of buzzards over dead meat, ready to destroy. "Nigga, God, your mama, your ex-best friend. . . . Can't nobody help you."

"What the fuck, Tony? I don't know what's going on!" Rich cried, his chin falling to his chest. He was exhausted. It had been eight hours since he'd been snatched from one of his side chicks' house in Richmond in the middle of the night. He had endured Jackson's abuse for four hours at this point.

Jackson stepped over and bent down in Rich's face.

"Nigga, you know what's going on. You stole from my brother, and you ain't know he was a Cartwright. You wrote your own death warrant," Jackson spat, the rubies and diamonds in his huge gold chain glinting at Rich like eyes of the devil.

Jackson was definitely the screw loose in the Cartwright family. Antonio's stomach churned at the thought of how many times he'd probably done something like this to their enemies.

"I . . . I . . . swear. . . . I don't—" Rich stammered through tears.

"Shut the fuck up!" Jackson boomed, stomping on Rich's bare feet with his Timberland boots. Everyone in the room cringed at the sound of the bones in Rich's toes cracking.

"Agh!" Rich howled, his words tumbling back down his throat like hard marbles.

"A'ight, a'ight, Jax." Antonio stepped between his brother and his battered friend.

"You ain't doing shit, and the nigga stole from you. I could give a fuck less about your broke ass, but *my* father wanted to send a message to everyone in the world that you're his," Jackson hissed, scowling at Antonio with so much disdain it was physically palpable.

"I'll take it from here," Antonio replied, his jaw tense.

"Well, handle it then," Jackson sneered, throwing his hands up. "Let us all see what the fuck you're made of, basketball boy."

Antonio had fire flashing in his eyes as he had a stare off with his brother. His nostrils flared as he prepared himself for what he knew he would have to do. He told himself that Rich had done him dirty and this was what the fuck he deserved. Antonio looked over at Hayden, and he nodded. Antonio stepped closer to his battered friend.

"Yo, Rich. I'm only going to ask you once. Where is the money? My money and all the money you took from the investors," Antonio said in a low, gruff voice that told the story of the conflict raging inside of him. "You ain't got no more chances."

Rich shook his head from left to right. He sobbed loudly, and his naked body quaked so hard it vibrated the chair.

Antonio sighed. He knew what this meant. He silently begged Rich to just answer the fucking question.

"The money, Rich?" Antonio's voice cracked, emotion evident in his words.

Hayden stepped over and handed Antonio a silver, long nose .45 Desert Eagle.

"Rich," Antonio rasped, fighting back tears. Suddenly he couldn't help but think back to their childhood.

Antonio and Rich had met as little kids in grade school. They were total opposites. It was probably why their friendship worked from day one. Rich was handsome, gregarious and always had other kids flocking around him, even at that young age. He was always that cool, smooth-dressing popular kid. Everybody liked him, and he always had the best of everything—clothes, sneakers, girls, clout. Antonio became endeared to Rich after he saved Antonio from the worst ass whooping of his life. After that, they became inseparable, like real blood brothers.

Antonio could never forget the day. It was sweltering hot outside, thanks to the heat wave that had hit the Bronx. There was an older dude everyone called Biggie, and he fucked kids up every day. He was the biggest bully in the state of New York, they were sure. He towered over all the kids and even some of the teachers. He was the true meaning of *menace to society.*

That particular day, Antonio had gotten into the sights of Biggie. Rich had walked up and found Biggie and his bully crew surrounding Antonio. They had taken Antonio's sneakers and his book bag. One kid had pushed Antonio to the ground, and Biggie had been moving in for the kill with this fake brass knuckles that he'd made out of thick, silver electrical tape. Antonio had his arm up, cowering and ready to die at Biggie's hands, when suddenly, Rich came out of nowhere and broke through the crowd that had formed to see Antonio's worst nightmare come true.

"Why the fuck y'all don't mess with dudes your own age and size?" Rich boldly stepped up and said in Biggie's face.

Antonio's eyes stretched so wide they ached at the edges. His mouth had hung open, too. Rich had stepped up like he was a grown man, and he didn't look scared at all. Biggie had immediately turned his sights to Rich.

"I know this shitty-face fuck nigga ain't talkin' to me," Biggie had growled, preparing his knuckles to meet Rich's face. But when Biggie moved in on Rich, Rich pulled his arm from behind his back and WHAM! Rich slammed a huge, jagged-edged rock into Biggie's head. Biggie had dropped in less than a second, his fat stomach and nasty butt crack exposed to the crowd.

"Who the fuck else wants to step up to get beat down?" Rich had yelled at the crowd. Antonio's shock hadn't faded from his face, but inside, he felt proud of Rich. Of course, none of the other bullies and cowards in Biggie's group stepped up to Rich. In fact, they had scattered like roaches when the lights come on. It had been clear to Rich and Antonio that none of them were shit without their fat, ugly bully of a leader.

Antonio had watched in shock and admiration as Rich walked over to him, extended his hand, and helped Antonio get up off the ground. Rich had a lot of friends, but he had suddenly become Antonio's most important friend.

Kids didn't tease Antonio anymore about being so lanky and skinny. The relentless names like, "starving African," "stick man," and "beanpole," suddenly just stopped after Rich accepted Antonio as his closest friend. Until then, Antonio had always had desperately low self-esteem, but being aligned with Rich back then had changed all of that.

"Yo! You taking care of this thief-ass nigga or what?" Jackson barked, snapping Antonio back to reality. "It's like you in a fucking daze and shit." Jackson turned to Hayden. "I knew this nigga wasn't no real Cartwright."

Antonio gripped the gun so tight now the veins in his wrist throbbed.

"I said *where is the money?*"

"I . . . I . . ." Rich stammered.

Antonio closed his eyes and pulled the trigger.

"Agh!" Rich squealed.

Antonio's head spun, and his hands shook like crazy.

"Where's my money?" he growled, his stomach in knots.

"Tone . . . man . . . it . . . it' s me," Rich begged, his words coming out in short puffs.

"You soft. This nigga is playing you," Jackson egged on. "He stole your whole life savings. Left your ass for dead where you can't even feed your bougie-ass wife. And you know where I found this nigga? Laid up in luxury with two bitches . . . one sucking his dick and the other one playing with his asshole. But you being Mr. Softee right now. I would've been done off this nigga. No false shots," Jackson pressed cruelly.

Another shot rang out. This time, blood splashed back, and Antonio tasted it in the back of his throat. He stumbled backward, the contents of his guts threatening to spew out of his mouth. He examined the mess in front of him. Antonio couldn't take it anymore. The smell and taste of his friend's blood, the idea that he might never see Rich again, and the idea of what he'd done, period. It was all too much. Antonio dropped the gun, turned around, bent over at the waist, and threw up.

Raucous laughter erupted behind him. "You aight?" Jackson asked through his laughter. "This shit is hilarious to me."

Hayden stepped over to Antonio and took the gun from him. "That's enough, Jax. Be easy."

Jackson spun around, pulled his gun out, smiled evilly, and leveled it at Rich's head. One last shot ended it.

Antonio dropped to his knees and gagged some more. He couldn't think straight. What the hell had he gotten into with this family?

"Thank me later, nigga," Jackson snarled next to Antonio's ear.

Unfazed, Hayden moved close to Antonio so that he could whisper in his ear. "You did fine. The first time is never easy, but trust me, it gets easier each time," Hayden said in an unsettlingly calm voice that sent chills down Antonio's spine.

Emil Cartwright stood behind a double-sided mirror watching his sons do what they needed to do. Emil hadn't taken his eyes off of Antonio—the one son he saw something in that he didn't see in the sons he had actually raised all of their lives. Emil took great satisfaction in watching Antonio take revenge on a man who had crossed him, even if the man was his friend. It took a big man to leverage revenge on a man you once considered as close as a brother. Emil knew that Antonio wasn't struggling because of the revenge; instead, he was struggling against the monster he knew lived inside of him and was afraid to unleash. Emil cracked a little smile. He knew this act of violence, once it really settled in to Antonio's psyche, would thrust him all the way into the business. Their real business.

"Yo, Pop." Jackson's loud voice interrupted Emil's deep thought. Something Emil hated. He cringed every time he had to deal with Jackson, his black stain son. Emil turned around slowly and mean-mugged Jackson. Emil wasn't happy with how his son had carried on.

"You see how your *son* bitched up? Crying and shit when that fuck nigga had stolen from him and shit," Jackson said, thinking he was impressing his father. "I'm telling you, that dude ain't cut out for this business. He's a square. He better go back and try to pick up that round rock and find a new team. Nigga ain't hard enough. He ain't got that extra thing. He soft as fuck . . ."

Emil held up his left hand, halting Jackson's incessant blabbering. He squinted his eyes and flexed his jaw. Jackson could tell his father was trying to hold onto his patience.

"What about what we discussed?" Emil asked, his jaw going stiff and his eyebrows dipping on his face.

Jackson could tell his father was in business mode. He quickly cut his losses and got down to the business at hand.

"It's just like I told you. That motherfucker Max King made a connection in Mexico that directly violated the agreement you had with him. I told you, the streets are talking, and the Cartwrights are looking weak these days. King made some connects and stepped directly on your toes. Matter of fact, he stomped on your toes," Jackson said. He walked closer to Emil, "We need to make a move sooner rather than later, or we gon' be losing millions per week."

Emil nodded. Jackson was a hothead, but he was Emil's best and most reliable street soldier. Emil loosened his tie and flexed his neck. Suddenly his expensive Armani suit and custom-tailored dress shirt felt too small and too scratchy against his skin. Just hearing the name Max King had that effect on him.

Max King was the quintessential old school black gangster. For decades before Emil emerged, Max had reigned over the drug, gambling, and escort rackets in New York. Max never liked Emil, and he once told Emil to his face that he viewed him as a threat. Emil was younger back then. It was in the early days when he was just a youngin' coming up in the game. Over the years, Max went out of his way to stop Emil from gaining leverage in the game, including: going head-to-head with Emil over territory, poisoning other gangsters against Emil, and using some powerful political connections to bring case after case against Emil. Max had been unsuccessful over and over again at taking Emil down. Despite Max's best efforts, Emil's businesses were booming on the legal and illegal sides. But, here Max was again, fucking with Emil's life.

"I'm telling you, Pop. You don't stop that motherfucker now, it's never," Jackson continued, circling around his father. Emil studied his other sons through the glass, his nostrils flaring.

"So, what was the outcome of the meetings? Did it make a dent in our bottom line?" Emil asked, trying hard to keep his cool.

"Hell yeah! I'm telling you, our distributors are all suspicious that our connects are drying up. Max put that word out on the street. I'm having a hard fucking time keeping them on board," Jackson continued, not mincing his words.

Emil didn't allow a lot of things to take him back to his days in the streets, but when that side of him was dragged up, it was apparent that he had a short fuse and a penchant for extreme violence when the situation called for it.

He stood brooding, his chest rising and falling rapidly. He stared out of the double-sided mirror and glanced out at the bruised, bleeding body on the other side.

"Make sure Antonio gets caught up to speed. He's a new face, and we will need him. Obviously, we are at war," Emil said evenly. "Make sure Hayden is made aware of my wishes. Antonio has to be the face in changing this tide. I didn't bring him into the fold for nothing. You know me better than that. I don't pay penance to anybody. . . not even someone claiming to be my son."

Chapter 6

Changing Faces

"G," Max King grunted, standing up to greet his old friend.

"Max," Gladstone Tillary sang, clapping his left hand on Max's shoulder. "It's been a while."

"Obviously, too damn long," Max said, motioning for Gladstone to sit down and eyeing the beautiful, young woman standing at his side. Max nodded, and one of his men rushed over and pulled out a chair for the statuesque woman. Gladstone pulled out his own chair.

"Max, this is Lori. Lori, this is Max, my old, old—" Gladstone began.

"That's enough 'olds,' you bastard," Max chimed with a slight hint of amusement in his tone. It was as much lightheartedness he was going to allow. He nodded at Lori but didn't greet her with words.

Max took his seat across from Gladstone and motioned for his henchmen to step back so they could have some privacy.

"What are you drinking?" Gladstone asked, picking up the drink menu and handing it to Lori. "And what's with the open meeting tonight? Something change?"

Roberto's was their usual meeting spot. Gladstone looked around and noticed that this time, Max hadn't closed the restaurant down for their meeting. It made

Gladstone slightly uncomfortable. He was more of a creature of habit. Max and Gladstone's childhood friend, Salvatore, owned Roberto's, and over the years, he had allowed Max and Gladstone to close down the restaurant so that they could dine in private along with their mistresses or other businessmen that Gladstone might not want to be seen with in public. In the past, Gladstone would enter through the front and Max would enter through the side or back. Salvatore never complained. He was loyal to both, as Max had given him his start-up money for his first restaurant, and Gladstone had helped put him on the front page by holding campaign events at his restaurants.

"Why the public meeting, suddenly?" Gladstone asked again, looking around. Although the restaurant wasn't crowded, it still unnerved him. He'd always preached to Max that the day they started changing up their routines was the day shit would go left in their dealings.

Max grunted and furrowed his brow. Gladstone knew him well enough to know that meant he was furious. Gladstone knew all about how Max had been losing a lot of money since he couldn't beat Emil Cartwright's drug prices, and the younger gamblers preferred Emil's gambling spots.

"We need to speak in private," Max said, his tone serious. "What I need to speak to you about is not for everyone's ears." Max's eyed Lori suspiciously.

"Trust me, Lori is fine," Gladstone assured. "She's my behind-the-scenes person. Who do you think handles the things the good upstanding senator can't? The dirty work . . . ." Gladstone said, putting his arm around Lori's shoulders and pulling her in for a kiss. She smiled at him but shot Max a dirty look.

"Suit yourself. I have nothing to lose . . . especially to some pussy," Max said, throwing his hands up and leaning into the table. "I'm not fucking happy about Cartwright getting off this last time." Max gritted his teeth. His chest started to heave.

Gladstone chuckled. "Are we back on this? I told you. We lodged an airtight case against him, but just like you, he has the money to buy his way out of shit," he said flatly. "It won't always work. Like a cat with nine lives, Emil's will run out sooner or later."

"The amount of money I've shelled out to you and your so-called people in high law enforcement positions to take down Emil . . . yet, he is still standing. Not only is he standing, but he's also getting stronger and richer. At my fucking expense," Max spat, a large vein at this left temple throbbing fiercely against his midnight skin.

Gladstone put his hands up in surrender. "Max . . . Max, c'mon. Be reasonable. You of all people know that none of us could've known that Emil would hire Penski, a former federal prosecutor, who knew all of the government's tricks before they used them. Penski is better than Johnny Cochran in his heyday. We had the judge in our pocket, and he did everything he could to sway the case in the government's favor. I mean . . . it was blatant. He was constantly ruling against Emil's defense's motions, objections, and he suppressed a bunch of the evidence favorable to Emil. It wasn't enough. Penski is just that fucking good."

"He should've done more," Max hissed.

"Do more and make it look obvious that Emil would win the case on appeal and have it overturned anyway? Then we wouldn't stand a snowball's chance in hell at getting him again. Now, at least, if we find the strongest dirt possible, something so concrete that it can't be contested, we can bring him down without looking like it's been a conspiracy against him all along," Gladstone explained.

Lori shifted in her seat.

"You okay, sweetheart?"

"I'm going to run to the ladies," she replied with a weak smile.

Gladstone followed her ass with his eyes.

"Mmm, mmm, mmm. She does it to me," he huffed.

Max looked at Gladstone and shook his head. "I have to get this motherfucker, Emil. With his hand in the motherfucking cookie jar."

"Red-handed is the only way at this point," Gladstone conceded. "Emil is a smart dude."

"Get that washed-up NBA son-in-law of yours to get the dirt on his sperm donor daddy," Max said facetiously.

"Antonio doesn't have a relationship with Emil. He barely knows him."

"I thought you were in the know, man," Max teased, leaning back like he had a deep, dark secret. "You mean to tell me the big badass senator doesn't know what's going on in his own family? Shit, they been keeping secrets from you, bruh."

Gladstone crumpled his face and tugged at his tie. The idea that something might be going on that he didn't know about immediately made his entire body feel hot.

"I'm more than in the know," he replied, sipping his drink.

"Oh yeah? So, what, y'all just don't discuss new jobs over Sunday dinner?" Max laughed.

"What are you getting at?" Gladstone shot back. Now he was pissed.

Max chuckled some more and took a long swig from his glass. He could see the tension building in Gladstone's face. That friendly yet competitive spirit was sitting right at the surface, threatening to spill over into an angry exchange.

"I thought you made sure you knew what was going on with your baby girl, Paige, since she married that former homeless kid," Max said, slapping Gladstone in his face with his words.

"Get to the fucking point," Gladstone shot back.

Max smiled wickedly. "Your son-in-law works for his daddy, Emil, now. And, I heard he is balls-in on all sides of the business. I would think that puts your precious Paige in jeopardy, wouldn't you? I mean, at best, it fucks with your reputation as a stand-up government representative, no? Shit, what will the world think when they find out Paige Tillary is married to the other side of the black mafia?"

Gladstone's jaw tensed, and his insides felt like he'd just swallowed a fiery torch. This had to be a lie! Antonio wasn't exactly who he'd envisioned for his daughter, but he certainly wasn't a gangster by any stretch. Gladstone used his polished politician skills to mask his feelings, but he knew Max could see right through it. "I'm sure you have it confused," Gladstone said evenly.

"Nah, I have it right. I thought that would motivate you to help me take Emil down. It's going to be a shit storm when it gets out that your daughter actually married into the Cartwright family and your golden boy, MVP, All-Star son-in-law is not the star everyone thought he was," Max said, his words like a million flies buzzing in Gladstone's ears.

Gladstone swallowed hard. There was no way that he could allow Emil to come along after all this time and muddy the Tillary name with his corruption and his reputation as a gangster in a suit.

Senator Tillary thought back to the first day that Paige had brought that no-good baller into his house.

She had just turned seventeen. He and her mother had spent thousands of dollars getting her ready for prom. The dress, the shoes, the hair and makeup—everything cost money, and Gladstone was happy to spend it if it meant his little girl would be happy. It seemed like just yesterday that she had walked down the stairs in their enormous mansion, a house that only generations and generations of money and political power could buy. She looked like royalty as she descended the curved staircase into the marble foyer. But she looked nervous.

"Daddy," she started, "I want you to meet my—" Paige cut herself off and Gladstone could see her hesitating. He was a protective father by nature. He knew what bad things were out there, what lay waiting for beautiful young girls like his daughter. He knew what she was trying to say. Lillian came into the foyer from the kitchen holding a glass of water, each for her and Gladstone. Their interactions as always were cool, but civil.

"Did you know that your daughter has a boyfriend?" asked Gladstone. He thought that Paige's nervousness was sweet. Lillian sipped her water dramatically.

"Does she now?" Lillian exclaimed in the style of a Southern belle. "When are we going to meet this impressive young man?"

Paige groaned at the thought of her parents interrogating Antonio the way they had interrogated every boy she had brought home before then. Usually them just showing up to meet her parents was a demonstration of bravery in and of itself. But two seconds after they made eye-contact with her naturally intimidating father, Paige was single once more.

"Daddy, please," Paige pleaded. The doorbell rang, and suddenly they were all out of time. It was time to face the music and the Senator. Paige model-walked over to the door, her puffy Carolina Herrera dress moving around her hips almost like it was independent of her body, her six-inch red bottoms clicking gracefully with each step. She swung the door open, and there stood Antonio. For the first time in her life, Lillian heard Gladstone gasp as he stood next to her.

"Mom, Dad," Paige started, "this is Antonio Roberts. We met at a basketball game a couple of months ago." Of course, this was a lie, but considering her having left the house on the night she actually met Antonio was also based on a lie, there wasn't much she could do now to fix the situation.

"Good evening, Mr. and Mrs. Tillary," Antonio greeted respectfully. He knew deep down that they could tell he didn't come from money. The tuxedo he had saved up to rent had a somewhat mothy smell to it, even after he doused himself in Yves Saint Laurent cologne. In the tuxedo's defense, it was Antonio's own fault he had gone to some small shop off of Grand Concourse. However, while Lillian made note of Antonio's biggest worry, Gladstone was stuck on something else.

It had taken Senator Tillary's catlike reflexes to not drop the glass he was holding when he saw Antonio Robert's face. Or should he say Emil Cartwright's eyes, and his lips, and his prominent cheekbones. There was no denying that one of the Cartwright bloodline had just stepped into his house.

"Roberts, you say?" Gladstone asked softly. Lillian looked at him, surprised. Gladstone was a lot of things, and soft was never one of them. He saw her reaction and raised his voice. "Where are you from, son?" he asked, already knowing the answer. Or so he thought.

Antonio didn't know what to say. Any answer he gave would be embarrassing. But there was no way around it.

"I grew up in the Patterson Houses," Antonio said, trying to hold himself up as straight as possible.

Gladstone Tillary didn't like being lied to. He told himself that he needed to talk to this boy alone. There was no way that a Cartwright would walk into his house uninvited without an ulterior motive.

"Lillian," said Gladstone, "why don't you take Paige upstairs so that she can grab her purse." Lillian, who knew her husband and all of his moods, took the hint. Paige groaned. She thought that he was about to do the classic Dad Talk, tell Antonio not to kiss her, leave room for Jesus and whatnot.

"Okay, dear," said Lillian. She shepherded Paige up the ornate staircase, closing the door to the master bedroom behind her. Antonio audibly gulped.

"So, Roberts, you said?" asked Gladstone, making his way toward a hall off the main foyer. Antonio dragged his feet to follow. They entered a kitchen with a ceiling higher than any Antonio had ever seen in someone's private home. The counters were the same marble as the floor in the entryway. Everything here was tailored to perfection. Antonio was out of his league. Gladstone made his way to the counter and pulled a bottle of wine out of the fridge, pouring what could only have been a deep and expensive red into a crystal glass.

"Yeah, just Antonio Roberts, no middle name," Antonio said awkwardly. He didn't know where to stand or what to do in this situation. Gladstone was drinking more money than Antonio had ever seen.

"What do your parents do for a living?" Gladstone said into his wine glass before his eyes darted up to meet Antonio's. They were standing farther away from each other than was normal and the tension only built.

"My mom is a hairdresser," Antonio said. It was only his embarrassment that kept him from adding the word "sometimes" at the end.

"And your father?" Gladstone asked quietly, pushing Antonio to what could only blow his cover. Antonio was embarrassed again but couldn't think of a quick enough lie.

"Honestly, sir, I've never met him."

Gladstone considered this. It wouldn't surprise him if Emil Cartwright had fathered some bastard child somewhere. But to leave him in poverty? There was no way that the Cartwrights would let that fly, there was no way Gladstone could know the truth. Either way, he wasn't going to let this broke ass kid from the projects come into his life, let alone his daughter's.

"How much money will it take?" said Gladstone.

"Excuse me, sir?" asked Antonio, wildly confused.

"How much money will it take for you to never see my daughter again?"

Antonio was floored. He thought stuff like this only happened in movies.

"With all due respect, sir," Antonio began, "Paige is worth more to me than any number you could give me."

Gladstone's face went dark. "Son, I don't give a fuck what you think my daughter is worth. My reputation is worth more," growled the Senator. It was then that Lillian entered the kitchen with Paige. Both men jumped. The two girls were laughing, but the tension still hung in the air.

"Ready to go, boo?" said Paige, happily. Antonio looked at Gladstone. If looks could kill, they would both be dead.

"Yeah, baby girl, I'm ready."

The sway of Lori's hips brought Gladstone back to reality. He and Max looked over at the same time and watched as she sauntered toward them. It was a welcome interruption.

"That is one beautiful distraction. I see why you don't know what's going on around you," Max said, flashing a smile. "Better close those nose holes and get your shit together."

Gladstone already knew Max and all of his men would have their eyes on Lori. She was hands down the most beautiful and sultriest out of all the extracurricular women that Gladstone had ever brought around.

Max could tell by the way Gladstone fawned over Lori and looked at her, he was into her heavy. Maybe a little too heavy.

"Just be careful. All it takes is one of them to bring you down," Max warned, nodding in Lori's direction. He was right. They'd both grown up in the shadows of the U.S. Capitol and had seen more than a handful of powerful politicians lose everything because they'd fallen blindly for a woman who wasn't supposed to be anything more than a short-lived fling.

"One of them you'd gladly take off my hands if I allowed it," Gladstone shot back. He knew Max cared about him, but he also knew Max was worried about losing the benefits that Gladstone's position afforded him. Gladstone sensed that Max was jealous and most likely wished he had Lori by his side.

Max threw his hands up. "Suit yourself, Senator," Max replied. "Just trying to help out an old friend, that's all."

"I'm Gladstone Tillary, and there ain't a bitch pretty enough to make me lose sight of my life and my family's name. Now, why don't you focus on finding that solid dirt on Emil, and not who I'm fucking?"

Max laughed loudly. "Same old Gladstone. Mr. Untouchable. Mr. Know-it-all. Mr. In-control."

Gladstone opened his mouth but didn't get a chance to speak.

"I'm back, baby," Lori sang, taking her seat.

"Back indeed," Max said snidely, dropping his fabric napkin on top of his half-eaten veal.

"I'll leave you two to it. I've already taken care of the tab for anything you order," Max said, standing up and buttoning his suit jacket. His henchmen moved to his side and prepared to exit the restaurant.

Gladstone stood up, plastered on a fake smile, and shook Max's hand vigorously. "I'll consider everything we spoke about and I'll have my people get in touch," Gladstone said, trying to make it seem all about business.

"You do that," Max said cryptically before he turned his back and walked off.

It was a shame that neither Max or Gladstone had noticed that someone had been watching them the whole time.

In his car outside of Roberto's, Jackson gritted his teeth. All this time, he had suspected that Antonio just popping up out of nowhere and trying to get into the family business was part of a larger plan. Seeing his supposed brother's father-in-law sitting down with their biggest rival only confirmed his suspicions. Somebody had to die for this.

"That fucking traitor," said the man sitting next to Jackson. He was one of their most trusted henchmen. As messy as Jackson was willing to get in the streets, when it came to family matters, things had to be handled much more delicately.

"You know what we have to do," said Jackson, his teeth still clenched.

"I know," said the man in the car as he cocked his gun.

***

Paige stood back and watched as cameras flashed and the paparazzi yelled out Michaela's name.

"Michaela! Michaela! This way! Smile, you look amazing!"

Paige shifted uncomfortably in Michaela's shadow, as usual. Paige's stomach churned, and suddenly she could feel the effects of her stilettos squeezing her feet. She hated heels. Always had.

"You look amazing! Where's Rod?" a popular internet tabloid reporter yelled out.

Michaela waved as she dazzled the crowd in a custom-made, floor-length beaded Michael Costello gown. Which of course made Paige feel like a tiny speck of dirt in her store-bought Nicole Miller dress, which, by the way, Michaela had encouraged her to purchase.

Paige felt smaller and smaller as she watched her best friend soak up the limelight. She didn't know how Michaela could love the spotlight this much. When Paige arrived, she was shocked to see the red carpet and all of the fanfare. She had been under the impression that the party for Rod was going to be a classy, private affair. Wrong. But with Michaela throwing it, Paige should've known better. Everything associated with Michaela was over the top, including her life. And this party.

Paige tip-toed away and exited the red carpet quietly. She had no desire to show up on the social media troll pages as the underdressed wife of washed-up basketball player Antonio Roberts. The bloggers had been relentless since Antonio got dropped, and everyone had now gotten wind of the Ponzi scheme that had left not only Antonio, but his many high-profile investors, broke. Not to mention, word got out about Antonio becoming an "executive" at Cartwright Enterprises. One notoriously messy blogger had made a meme with Antonio on the left and Al Pacino on the right that read *"Michael or Fredo Corleone, which one?"* Paige had heard Antonio cursing about it to his brother Hayden. Life was definitely changing for all of them.

Paige navigated her way through the throngs of photographers and headed toward the entrance. She left Michaela still smiling, sauntering, and swinging her hair. All eyes were on Michaela, just how she liked it.

Paige still couldn't believe that just a year ago she was living the high life just like Michaela. Paige couldn't have imagined she would've been thrust into this fake, pretend life she was portraying now. She surely wasn't looking forward to seeing the girls tonight, or her mother and father for that matter.

Paige headed toward the entrance of the star-studded affair. She smiled some more, showing off her gleaming white teeth. It was all she could do to not feel ashamed of herself. She was kind of jealous of how fiercely independent Michaela was. Being a kept woman had bored Michaela, but it was really the only life Paige knew. Michaela wasn't about sitting around waiting for a man to spoon-feed her when he felt like it. Her husband, Rod, had had his share of infidelities and bad acts, but none of it seemed to sway Michaela off her determined path.

"Paige! Girl, you look beautiful!"

Paige whirled around to find Koi beaming with her arms extended in front of her. Paige rolled her eyes in her mind, but still smiled and embraced Koi with a warm hug.

"You look beautiful too!" Paige lied. Nothing Koi ever wore was flattering on her. Tonight was no different. The bright yellow, two-sizes-too-small bandage dress Koi had chosen made her look like a stuffed Chiquita banana.

"This girl Michaela absolutely out did herself," Koi sang as she opened her arms wide for emphasis.

Paige had to agree. The room glowed with black and silver—Rod's team colors. The centerpieces sparkled with beautiful bouquets of black-dyed hydrangeas, silver roses, and, beautiful, big leaf, pure white calla lilies sitting on top. The glittery silver sequined tablecloths and floor-to-ceiling drapery was a personal touch that screamed money, money, money.

"Well, you know how Michaela does. She has to show the world that she's happy and rich," Koi replied with a chuckle. She grabbed Paige's wrist. "C'mon. Let's go find the other girls and some damn drinks," she said, dragging Paige along.

Paige noticed Koi's husband, the famous . . . or infamous, Damien Armstrong, former criminal turned pastor of Full of Life Ministries. Of course, he was already surrounded by a bunch of women who definitely weren't Koi's friends. But, at least Damien was there, which was more than Paige could say about Antonio.

Paige had her winning smile plastered on her face, although she still wanted to turn around and go home. She hadn't heard from Antonio, and she'd waited as long as she could before she would've been way late to Michaela's party. In the end, Paige had left home without Antonio, and until that minute he still hadn't returned any of her calls. It had been weighing on Paige's mind lately how Antonio had been putting his new "business" first. When he was home, all he did was sleep because he'd been out at after-hours meetings so late. All he spoke about now was Emil, Hayden, and Jackson. It was crazy to her how easily they'd become number one in his life. Paige had played second fiddle to the demands of Antonio's basketball career, and now here she was again, shucking and jiving, trying to appear happy when her insides were raging with anxiety, worry, and sadness.

Paige couldn't remember fake smiling and artificially giggling this much in a long time. With both of her big toes numb from her heels, Paige finally sat down on one of the beautiful black suede couches and picked up a flute of champagne. She'd been drinking more and more, so gone were the days when she politely declined alcohol with a shy, "I don't drink." Paige took a sip and checked her watch. She sighed. *Why is Antonio constantly making me out to be a liar lately?* she thought. She had told Michaela and everyone else that he was coming. Her jaw rocked as she picked up another champagne flute.

"Wait one damn minute. What exactly happened to the Paige I know that doesn't drink?"

Paige looked up to find Casey standing over her, smiling, with her cute cheek dimples making her look way more innocent than she was.

"That Paige has left the building," Paige replied with a chuckle. Then she lifted the second glass to her lips.

"Well, shit. I'm glad. You know I'm a big proponent of women loosening up and not acting like they can't drink and have fun just because they're married and shit," Casey said.

Before Paige could say anything else, she and Casey both paused at the sound of loud voices coming from behind them. Paige turned her head, and Casey turned her entire body at the group of women huddled together around another beautifully dressed woman. They looked as if they were preparing her for a war, as she handed one her purse and another her earrings.

"Oh God, what is about to happen?" Koi said, rushing toward Paige and Casey.

"I know that face," Casey whispered, pulling out her cell phone, ready to record.

They all watched as the girl stormed toward Rod and Michaela, who'd just made their grand entrance. Paige stood up and swallowed hard. Nothing good could be coming out of this.

"Let's—" Paige started, but it was too late.

"Rod! Rod!" the beautiful young woman yelled loudly, aggressively waving at the couple.

Casey moved forward, her phone recording everything. Koi gasped and put her hands on her cheeks like a real-life screaming face emoji. Paige stood, frozen, her feet feeling rooted to the floor.

"You just going to be up in here with this bitch after you told me you left her?" the girl screamed. A collective round of gasps and grumbles rose and fell over the crowd. The girl's overdone blond-with-black-roots, Beyonce-length weave, swung as her head rocked from side to side. She was not backing down, and she advanced forward so fast no one in the crowd could keep a good grip on her. Her group of friends held her down and made sure she got to her target.

"Oh. My. God," Paige finally managed. She kicked off her shoes and started toward the melee.

"You have to let this one play out," Casey said, holding Paige's arm while she continued recording with her other hand.

Paige twisted away and acted like she didn't hear Casey. She raced forward. Even with the music blaring, Paige was sure everyone in the party knew what was happening at that point.

"So, Rod, are you going to act like you don't know me?" the young woman spat, standing toe-to-toe with Rod, pointing a bedazzled nail in his face.

Michaela stepped forward. "Excuse me . . . just who the fuck do you think you are?" She pushed the girl in her chest.

"I'm his gir—" she couldn't even finish her sentence before Michaela slapped her so hard a tiny bit of spit flew from her lips.

Paige wiggled through the cell-phone-recording and fight-video-hungry crowd.

"Michaela! Don't!" Paige yelled, grabbing Michaela before she could do any more damage. She had seen firsthand over the years the destruction Michaela was capable of with her bare hands.

"Move, Paige. I'm going to show this little bitch what it means to be bold," Michaela barked, kicking the air toward the girl. The gloves were off. Fuck a gown; Michaela was ready to destroy.

The young girl smirked. "You might be his wife, but he told me he hasn't fucked you in years! He wants to be with me, and I am pregnant! Rod, tell her!"

Michaela's head rocked back like the girl's words were an actual punch in her face. "What? Oh, no bitch," Michaela screamed. She moved so fast that Paige didn't have time to grab her.

"I'm going to kill you. You ruined my party," Michaela shrieked. She was on top of the girl, ripping at her weave and her dress. It was like something out of a movie.

"Rod, are you going to do something?" Paige screamed.

It was as if Rod had been shocked frozen. He finally moved to break up the fight.

"Bitch, you ruined my night," Michaela screeched as Rod finally picked her up. Michaela's legs moved wildly like she was riding an invisible bike. She clawed at Rod's thick arms as he tried to keep her away from his tacky mistress.

That was enough. Paige's insides exploded with heat, and she rounded on the girl's group of friends. "Get your dirty-ass friend and get the fuck out of here before you all go to jail. This is an invite-only party and I don't know how you rats got in, but I definitely know how you'll be removed," Paige said through her teeth. It was an uncharacteristic move for her, but the one thing she didn't want to see was her best friend hurting. Michaela's beautiful face was a mess of smudged makeup and tears.

"Rod, you haven't seen the last of me. You and your bitch wife will be sorry for the day you did this to me," the girl screamed.

Before Paige could react again, security finally swarmed the area and the girl was hoisted up like a ragdoll.

"Get off of me! Rod, tell them to get off of me. I'm your girl . . . remember? Tell them," the woman hollered, kicking and screaming as she was carried toward the exit.

"Can you believe this shit?" Casey asked excitedly.

A little too excitedly for Paige's liking. "She's our friend, Casey. This is not the time for you to be thinking about shit for your show," Paige said, disgusted, storming away from Casey.

Paige rushed into the bathroom, where a crowd had already formed around Michaela.

"Everybody out," Paige yelled. "And take your cell phones with you! I'm sure you all are not as concerned as you say you are."

There was a bunch of grumbling and mumbling, but most of the women began filing out of the bathroom.

Michaela turned toward Paige, tears streaming down her face like Niagara Falls. She smiled weakly, shook her head, and ran her hands down the front of her gown.

"Are you okay?" Paige asked, almost whispering.

Michaela waved her hand and laughed, despite the contradictory sadness showing up on her face. "Yeah, girl. That's nothing. She's probably a fan. You understand, right? From Antonio's days," Michaela said, playing it off.

Paige rocked on her feet. It was a low blow from Michaela, but Paige remained calm. Suddenly, her insides were raging. Why did Michaela always need to drag her down when things weren't going right for Michaela. She'd been doing that since they were younger. Paige cleared her throat and held tight to her composure. She knew Michaela was hurting.

"You want me to have the DJ announce that the party is over?" Paige managed.

"Hell no!" Michaela laughed. "I spent way too much money on this. I needed this," she said.

Paige stared at Michaela with sympathy.

"We needed this," Michaela's voice cracked.

"Oh, Mick," Paige said, pulling Michaela in for a hug.

Michaela melted against Paige and sobbed. They both sobbed. Life was so different now for both of them. And, in that moment, they both knew it would never be the same again.

Paige was on the verge of hysteria all the way home. It seemed to take forever. As soon as she pulled her Benz truck into the circular driveway, her heart sank. Antonio wasn't home.

"This bastard doesn't show up to the party and ain't home either? Real stand up, Antonio. Real fucking stand-up guy you are," Paige grumbled as she exited the car.

Once inside, Paige kicked off her heels and wiggled her toes. Too much had happened tonight. Her head felt a little dizzy from the champagne, and her stomach felt nauseous as she continued to think about what had happened to Michaela. How fucking embarrassing!

The smell of lavender reached Paige's senses and reminded her that at least she still had the comfort of her luxurious home to come back to. Antonio was gone all of the time, but it was for a good cause. There was no way Paige could give up what she had become accustomed to.

She shook her head. "You're doing it again, Paige. Making excuses for him. He wasn't there because he's a fucking loser, not because he wants to keep you in this house," she spoke to herself.

Paige climbed the winding staircase and gently crept down the long hallway at the top of the stairs. When she got to the third door, she smiled at the little wooden basketball-shaped name-plate hanging on the door. She carefully turned the knob and pushed the door open. Her heart melted as she stood and watched the rise and fall of her baby boy's tiny chest.

"You're the only man that matters anyway," Paige whispered. She tiptoed out of the room and shut the door. If she never had the love of any other man, her son Christian's little hugs and kisses would be enough to last her a lifetime.

"You up? Hey, Paige, you up?"

Paige groaned and pulled the fluffy down comforter over her head.

"I'm sorry I didn't make it there. Some shit went down and I . . ."

Annoyed, Paige took the covers off of her head and squinted in the darkness.

"What do you want, Antonio? I'm sleeping."

"I can see that, but I just wanted to tell you what happened," he said, his voice cracking like it did whenever he was guilty.

"Whatever, Antonio. I'm so over it all, it's not even funny," Paige said, popping up in the bed with her face folded into a scowl. "It's really funny how you can be there for your *new* family but fuck your *real* family."

"Here we go again," Antonio rolled his eyes. "Do you think shit is always about you, Paige? I'm telling you I need to speak to you about something important, and you're worried about the appearances again?" Antonio snapped.

Paige's eyebrows went low on her face. "What, Antonio? I'm listening." She sighed and rolled her eyes. It was always about him.

"Forget it," he said, slumping down on the side of the bed. "Forgive me for thinking I can speak to my wife about serious shit."

Paige threw her legs over the side of the bed and stood up. "I didn't say you couldn't talk to me, Antonio," Paige said, softening her tone. There she was, people-pleasing again and putting his feelings before her own.

"I think Rich is dead," he blurted.

"What?" Paige rasped, barely able to get the word out. "What are you talking about?"

Antonio lowered his face into his hands. "Paige, I know he's dead. I . . . I . . ."

Paige flopped down on the bed next to him, her legs seemingly giving out. "You what?" she whispered.

Antonio let out a loud sob. It was as if the reality of his new lifestyle had finally caught up to him. His body melted against Paige's. She could feel the tension easing as she held onto him. He was a like a balloon full of air being deflated.

"I didn't stop it," he croaked. "I was there, and I didn't stop it. He was always there for me. He made a mistake. I did it, Paige. I did it."

"Shh. Don't talk," Paige said softly. "It's not your fault. Don't talk about it."

"You have to hear me out. I need to tell someone this, and you're the only person who could never testify against me. The Cartwrights are into some heavy shit, and I need to be a part of it for us, but I want you to start making sure we have a plan . . . if ever we need it. We need an escape plan," Antonio said with feeling.

Paige closed her eyes and shuddered just thinking about what he was saying. She was terrified, but she wanted to be there for him.

"I will always be here for you, Antonio. For us," she said, unsure if she even meant it. "And just remember, if we ever need it, my family is always around. My father is a lot of things, but he has our backs."

Antonio let out a long breath, mixed with sobs. Paige knew he hated when she brought up her father and how her family could bail them out, but she wanted him to know that it was always an option.

"I'm never going to go to your father for help over getting my hands dirty to feed my family," Antonio replied. "I just need to know that I have you in my corner . . . no matter what happens."

Paige shook her head. "Okay," she said weakly. "But just be careful."

Antonio turned toward her and looked her in the eyes. "Paige, I want to do what's best for us, but I know the more I move up, the more I'm going to need to change faces. Just know that I love you and Christian more than life."

"I know," Paige said, though she wasn't too confident that she believed him.

Michaela sat, sobbing, and thinking through what had happened, and she wondered how she had fallen this far. There she was, on Paige's couch, crying over a $10 bottle of wine now that both of them were, for all intents and purposes, broke.

"It's not your fault," Paige said, walking up to her.

It had been a week since the fiasco at Rod's birthday party, and his mistress's pregnancy had been confirmed. As far as the tabloids were concerned, their relationship had ended, and Michaela didn't know if it was worth her reputation to try and salvage it now that things were so far gone.

"How is it not my fault?" cried Michaela. She was a little drunk, and her emotions had gotten the best of her. Their entire relationship, Rod had cheated on her. To be perfectly honest with herself, the way she and Rod had met involved him cheating on his first wife. Paige had told her at the time not to mess with a married man, especially a baller, because there is nothing in a woman that they wouldn't find replaceable with another one.

"You can't keep a man that doesn't want to be kept, girl, it just doesn't work," said Paige. And who better than her to know? The cheating had, for lack of a better word, broken her. And when it happened, she and Michaela were essentially in the same position, but with their roles reversed: Paige crying and Michaela stroking her head instead. It was crazy the lengths that women have to go to protect each other from the damage that men do. Even watching Michaela go through it now, reminded her of how much Antonio's infidelity had hurt her all those years ago.

"You're so lucky you have Antonio," muttered Michaela before hiccuping. Paige sneakily grabbed the wine bottle away from her.

"What do you mean?" said Paige, "He's cheated on me before too, you were the one that told me to give him another chance." She was so confused by Michaela's mindset. She seemed to go from hot to cold, and back again, with no type of explanation.

"Antonio is different, though," she choked through her constant stream of tears. "You can tell he really loves you."

Paige looked at the top of her friend's head as it lay in her lap. She was wondering if maybe she did have a point. From the moment they had met, Antonio had made it clear to everyone around them that he was obsessed with Paige. Everything about her. He thought she was beautiful, and smart, and funny. When he looked at Paige, he didn't see her money or status, he just saw her. Even though he had had his moment of infidelity, love would always win out. Paige knew that the way Rod and Michaela had started up had been less about love, like Antonio and Paige shared, and more about what would look the best in the papers. Like Michaela, Rod loved knowing that his reputation as a stud would be solidified by marrying an old-money girl. And Michaela, with her tendency to want to one up Paige, also wanted to be able to tell people that she married a pro-athlete. With all this in mind, Michaela was probably right, Paige's situation with Antonio was different. but it was still weird the way that Michaela rode for him.

"You can't think like that, girl, you'll only hurt your own feelings," Paige said. Michaela's head was still in her lap, and she was petting her hair like you do with an infant who has just finished a tantrum and has started to calm down. There was a mixture of sweat and tears beaded up on her forehead, and if Paige didn't love her so much, she would have stopped, because it was a little gross. But taking care of Michaela was one of Paige's favorite things to do, the one place that she couldn't be one-upped.

"It's okay, Paige, everyone knows it," Michaela responded. And then she laughed. She lifted her head off of Paige's lap so fast, she almost threw her wine across the room. Paige was in shock. Clearly, something in Michaela had broken. Her tears and laughter mixed together until she was almost screaming.

"Michaela, Jesus, what's wrong?" Paige yelled over her friend's nervous breakdown, standing up from the couch. Michaela calmed down into giggles and looked up at Paige, heavy eyeliner streaming down her face. She looked like an oversized raccoon and was somehow still so beautiful.

"Because," she said. "This is our whole life."

"What do you mean?" asked Paige.

"We've spent our whole lives caring for these men. Building them up. And look at what they've done to us." Michaela had stopped crying and was looking down at her hands that she held together like she was praying. "We have nothing without them."

Chapter 7

Moving In and Moving Up

Antonio laughed at Emil's corny joke. "Man, you're one funny old man."

Emil clapped him on the shoulder and smiled. "I hope you're feeling at home here."

Antonio nodded his approval. His relationship with Emil was blossoming. In Antonio's eyes, Emil was happy to have all three of his sons working for him. He'd been pointing out to Hayden and Jackson how well business was doing since Antonio had come aboard. Sometimes, Emil made Antonio uncomfortable when he sang his praises. Antonio knew Jackson didn't like Emil to shower Antonio with praises at all.

"Whose turn was it to buy lunch?" Emil asked loudly as he took his seat for his weekly lunch meeting with his sons.

"Mine, why?" Jackson replied.

"Just asking," Emil said, winking at Antonio. They started laughing.

"Fuck is that supposed to mean?" Jackson snapped, looking from his father to Antonio and back again.

Emil held up his hand. "It was a little joke between me and my son. Let's get to the business at hand. Let's start with the numbers. Hayden?"

Hayden moved uncomfortably in his seat and fiddled with the stack of papers in front of him.

"Um, well . . ." Hayden stammered.

Antonio, Jackson, and Emil all looked on, confused.

"Spit it the fuck out," Jackson shouted.

"The intake collected from the gambling spots Antonio is in charge of does not match the books," Hayden said, clearly uncomfortable with what he had to say.

Antonio sat up in his chair. "Wait, what? That's impossible."

Emil raised an eyebrow at Hayden. "Are you sure it was Antonio's spots?"

"I'm positive," Hayden said firmly. "I did the count over and over."

"That's bullshit!" Antonio spat. He was shocked by Hayden, who'd always seemed to have his back.

"Nah, somebody must've dipped in after the collection," Jackson said, shockingly intervening on Antonio's behalf.

"Don't fucking gang up on me! I'm telling you what was in the count!" Hayden barked, angry that Jackson would dare go against him for Antonio. "How the fuck do you know that it wasn't him? It damned sure wasn't me!"

"Well, nigga, something ain't kosher here at all. I helped with the count, I sealed the bags myself and rode with bruh to drop it off," Jackson continued.

Hayden's eyes flashed with fire. Suit or not, he wasn't about to let them flip this on him for Antonio's sake. He'd been the one to accept Antonio into the fold before Jackson, and now they were flipping it on him.

Emil stood up. "Enough. A simple solution to this is that Hayden needs to check his people, because they must've pocketed the money that they were being paid to clean."

Hayden slapped his hands on the table in front of him and shot up from his chair. Seeing his father agree with the black sheep son and the illegitimate son fueled Hayden's anger even more. "Fuck all of y'all," Hayden hissed.

Antonio wasn't all that shocked. Being a star athlete his entire life, Antonio had dealt with jealous haters for a long time. He easily recognized the jealousy in his own brother's eyes. All the while he thought Jackson was his problem, but now, he knew neither brother was that keen on him being around. He quickly and quietly made a mental note to stay one step ahead of everyone in the room. Or so he thought.

Blu Lounge was a nightclub located on the west side of the Bronx. They called it the Blu. The club was housed in a nondescript, red brick building that resembled an old factory. It was a holdover from the days when Emil cleaned his dirty money through the legitimate club scene. After a young girl had been shot during a party fight gone bad, Emil had been forced by the Feds to shut it down. Now it was just used for important meetings with Emil's distributors.

A dude named Kenneth Barnes technically owned the Blu, although, on paper, it used to be one of the legitimate businesses Emil still held majority ownership in. Thinking back, Antonio remembered coming to the Blu one time to party and celebrate a win with his basketball team. Admittedly, he didn't remember much about that night, especially after drinking almost an entire bottle of D'usse.

Antonio felt slightly exhausted. He had tossed and turned the previous night after his brother Hayden had accused him of stealing. Suddenly, he felt like he had no loyalties from Hayden nor Jackson. When Emil had told Jackson and Hayden to bring Antonio to the meeting, something inside of Antonio's gut didn't feel good about it.

Still, Antonio was there. So far, he had amassed about thirty thousand dollars in cash and another twenty thousand in treasury bills. Hardly enough to provide for Paige and for them to continue to live comfortably.

If Antonio had any doubts about being there, they went out the window when he reminded himself about his financial situation. He sat behind the wheel of his burgundy Escalade, the first car he'd gotten when he became famous. He'd brought out the old school to remind himself of how far he'd come.

His eyes were covered in dark shades, and the gun on his hip brought him a small bit of comfort. Antonio had sat in the cut and watched at least twelve dudes, some in business suits and others in jeans and hoodies, file into the Blu. Some came in groups and others solo, but they all seemed well acquainted with one another. Antonio figured he'd wait for Hayden and Jackson to arrive before he made himself known.

Antonio gave himself a mental pep talk. *You ain't got shit to lose. Watch out for the snakes. Don't trust none of them. Get what you came for . . . what's owed to you.* He wasn't sure what he would encounter inside, but he did know he wasn't going to be weak in front of his brothers ever again. Antonio felt something changing inside of him. And, he didn't know if it was for the better.

He stepped out of the car and immediately noticed that his legs were shaky like strands of cooked pasta. He smoothed the material of his Armani suit, which he'd worn just so he'd remind Jackson and Hayden that he still resembled Emil the most. He was Emil's son, whether they liked it or not.

As he walked confidently, his hard-bottom Christian Louboutin loafers sounded off on the uneven cobblestones. The way he was dressed sent the message he wanted to convey—he was there to be about his, and Emil's, business. Antonio had the right to be there too.

The clear plexiglass door handles opened effortlessly.

Inside, a slender man came rushing toward Antonio.

"Nah, we closed," the man said, ready to force Antonio back out the door.

Antonio removed his glasses so the man could see his face fully. His nerves were on edge, but he managed to suppress the sheer nervousness well.

The man's eyes went wide like he'd seen a ghost.

"Oh, shit. You . . . you're Tony Roberts from the . . . I'm so sorry. I—I didn't think," the man stammered, an awkward, nervous smile pasted on his lips.

Antonio chuckled. "It's all good. Where is the meeting?" he asked.

The man's head snapped up, seemingly surprised. "You here for the . . . I mean . . . you play ball. . . ."

"I'm here for the meeting with the Cartwrights. My brothers," Antonio said.

"Oh, shit. Um, right this way," the man said, his words rushed and quivery. He ushered Antonio up a flight of stairs and down a long hallway. There were two heavy wooden doors at the end of the hallway.

"Right in here," the man urged, pointing Antonio in the direction of the forbidden underworld realm. "Man . . . can I get your autograph before you leave?"

"I got you."

Antonio took a deep breath and turned both knobs simultaneously, opening the French doors. The bustling and noisy scene before him seemed to pause like a movie. All the men inside the room turned toward the door and stood stock-still, jaws hanging wide. Antonio felt hot all over. He felt suspended in time, his feet seemingly rooted in place.

Jackson was the first to react. He jumped up from the end of a shiny, dark wood table and rushed toward Antonio.

"If it ain't the man of the hour?" Jackson said in the same smart-ass-mouth way he said everything. In all the time since Antonio had been working with his family, Jackson had never been this enthusiastic about seeing him. It made Antonio feel slightly uneasy.

"Either I'm looking especially good today, or you dudes got a thing for dudes. Which one is it?" Antonio asked, laughing.

"This is our brother, Antonio," Hayden announced, moving to Antonio's side. He still hadn't apologized for that little stunt he'd pulled. Antonio never thought he'd see the day when he felt better about being around Jackson than he did being around Hayden.

"Brother, what the fuck kinda game is this? Ain't that the motherfucking basketball player Tony Roberts?" one of the dudes in the room shouted.

"Shut the fuck up, Grim," Jackson yelled. "We said this is our fucking brother."

The room went silent as the occupants watched Antonio so hard he felt the heat of their gazes burning him up.

"Now, this nigga is here at the request of my father. He's here to learn about our business dealings. If somebody in this room thinks they got a problem with him being here, they better think again," Jackson gritted, his words forceful enough to send chills through the room. A wave of groans traveled the length of the table. Antonio had seen some of the men before at events he'd gone to with his brothers, but many were new faces.

What the fuck am I doing here? They can all shoot me down right here in this room! Though the thought flitted through his mind, Antonio knew that he couldn't back out of the meeting now.

"Well, don't mind me. Let's get started," Antonio said boldly, sitting down at the end of the table. Each man turned to each other incredulously. He was all in now. There was no turning back. No showing signs of weakness either.

A dark-haired Hispanic man slammed his hands on the table and stood up so fast he sent his rolling chair into the wall behind him.

"Oye, cabrones, yo no tengo tiempo para estas pendejadas. Yo no estoy aquí para ver un pinche juego de basketball?" *Listen, motherfuckers, I don't have time for this bullshit. I'm not here to watch a fucking basketball game.* He spoke to another man who stood at the back of the room defiantly.

"We don't just allow outsiders into our business meetings!" someone else at the end of the table complained. Two more men stood up, their faces stony. The room was abuzz with gruff protests now.

Hayden's face flushed and sweat danced down his sideburns.

"Everybody just calm down," Hayden pleaded, frazzled. He turned back toward Antonio. "We will take care of this."

"Nah. I'm not here for a basketball game that's for sure," Antonio announced loudly. The Hispanic man looked shocked that Antonio had understood his insult. "But I will say this, I'm here to find out about the dealings of my father's business. I know that you all respect the Cartwright name, and we are the supplier here, and none of you have the high-level connections that our family has. We hold the key to your livelihoods, so you better learn how to play ball . . . and not fucking basketball," Antonio said.

His words dropped like tiny bombs around the room. They all knew he was right. Each man in that room was dependent on the Cartwrights like a baby depends on its mother's milk. In their business, Antonio had come to learn, dudes in those seats had better learn to obey him first, react second.

"Oh, shit! A nigga getting some balls," Jackson joked. He was the only one in the room smiling though.

"Let's get to the business at hand. We are moving to a new connect. And my father gave the name to me. Even Hayden and Jackson didn't know this," Antonio announced.

The room erupted again. This time it wasn't low grumbles and mumbles, it was all out pandemonium.

"What the fuck?" Jackson whispered, pulling Hayden's arm. "Did you know about this shit?"

"Obviously fucking not. I'm just as surprised as you," Hayden whispered back harshly. "Pop is playing games. Dangerous games."

Antonio held up his hand. "Let's all talk. I think you'll all want to hear what I have to say."

A hush fell over the room like a soft blanket on a sleeping infant. Each man slowly took his seat, a captive audience.

Something tingled inside of Antonio's gut. He felt a surge of confidence and power enter his bloodstream. Is this what it was like to be a Cartwright? He couldn't front, the rush was better than stepping onto a basketball court and hearing a crowd cheer for you. This rush was different, like when you had forbidden sex as a teenager. So good, yet so bad.

Clearing his throat, Antonio began laying out the things Emil had told him to say, with authority.

Antonio had been told that he needed to give Jackson leash with a little bit of length, but not too much that he

would think he could run free. It had been an unprec-
edented move by Emil. One that even Antonio didn't
understand himself. He couldn't lie . . . he felt super
powerful.

When the men filed out of the room, Hayden and
Jackson remained so they could chat separately.

Jackson stood so close to Antonio he could feel the
heat of his breath on his lips.

"I know you may have fucking convinced Pop that
you can be trusted, but I don't trust you. You have no
fucking idea what you're getting yourself into. You're not
about this life, nigga. What the fuck was that all about?"
Jackson gritted, baring his teeth. Jackson was showing
his spoiled brat ways and letting Antonio know just how
threatened he felt.

"Look, man. I'm doing what Pa . . . I mean . . . what
Emil asked me to do. If you got a problem with the
decisions being made, you need to take that shit up with
him." Antonio wasn't going to back down. Now more
than ever, he needed to stand his ground. He couldn't
front, his insides were churning with nervousness.

Emil had put him in a fucked-up predicament. Why
him? Why had Emil chosen him to announce the new
supplier? That was always Jackson's role in the family.
Hayden was the clean business guy, who sometimes had
to get his hands dirty. He was the square that Emil could
put in front of a group of legitimate businessmen and feel
good about it. But, him, Antonio . . . where did he fit in?
He still couldn't figure it out. Shit wasn't exactly making
sense.

"Stepping into this business is not something you want
to do. You don't know these dudes and you don't know
shit about this business. Once you're in, you can never
get out," Jackson gritted, his eyes lit with animosity.
Antonio thought about what Jackson was saying. He

thought about Paige, her family, their reputation, their son. He mulled over Jackson's words. But, in the end, it didn't matter. Emil had chosen him. The arrangement had been made, and if he didn't stick with it, it could result in multiple casualties. So he really had everything to lose either way.

"What did you expect me to do? Tell your father no? Walk away from his connections, all of his business, and money? Leave everything to you and Jackson? Run away when I've been running all of my life? Do I look stupid to you? Last I checked, I'm just as much a Cartwright as both of you," Antonio said pointedly.

Jackson closed his eyes and scrubbed his hands over his face. It was all he could do not to punch Antonio in the face. There was no winning this argument. Jackson put his hands up in front of him in surrender. He had to get Antonio on his side. It was the only way he could get what he needed. But once he did, all of them would be sorry.

"Listen," Hayden said, stepping forward. Both Antonio and Jackson glared at him. "We can sit here and run over this all night, but Pop made the decision." Then he turned his full attention to Antonio. "I just need you to understand that running numbers and the other stuff we've exposed you to this far, is *not* the same as running this business," Hayden warned. "I'm sure Pop thinks you're cut from the same cloth as he is, but this side of the business, it's no place for a soft, orphan foster kid turned celebrity basketball star who is a total amateur." His words felt like an open-handed slap on Antonio's face.

"Don't ever mention my childhood out of your mouth again. You grew up how you grew up, and I grew up how I grew up. . . . Leave it at that," Antonio said calmly, clearly fighting the rage inside.

Jackson shoved his hands into his pockets and balled his fists until his knuckles throbbed. Hayden bit down into his jaw until his head hurt. Neither was prepared to share the possibility of becoming the boss with anyone, much less the son of their father's whore.

Antonio stepped out of Jackson's Range Rover and slammed the door behind him. Jackson handed his keys to the eager-for-a-tip valet standing in front of the towering skyscraper in midtown Manhattan. Antonio glanced back at the caravan of black SUVs that had followed them down from the Bronx. Jackson nodded at his little street dude, who sat shotgun in the front passenger seat of the first vehicle. Antonio didn't bother to look back at any of the passengers of the other three heavily tinted vehicles. Antonio and Jackson had exchanged hardly any words while in the truck on their way to meet the new connect in a high rise in the heart of New York City.

Antonio tugged at this suit lapels and straightened himself out. He looked at his brother and mentally shook his head, partly in disgust and partly in empathy. Jackson was just a hood dude at his core, nothing could change it. Not even a father like Emil.

Antonio noted the stark differences between himself and Jackson, from the way they dressed, talked, looked, and carried themselves. Antonio knew he would never have chosen to wear a pair of flashy-pocketed Balmain jeans, a bright ass Gucci T-shirt, a leather Balmain jacket, and red Balenciaga boots, to an important business meeting. Antonio was much classier than that. He'd chosen a smoke gray Armani suit, similar to one he'd seen Emil wear; a perfect satin pocket square; a pristinely pressed, crisp white French cuff shirt with diamond monogrammed cufflinks worn open at the collar; and on his feet, a pair of black suede Salvatore Ferragamo loafers. Antonio's outfit exuded class and sophistication. When he looked at his brother, it was all hood nigga vibes.

Antonio looked around the lobby of the building and thought about Paige. She would love to live in a fancy building like this one. He'd been thinking about her a lot. He was deep in the trenches now, and if she knew everything, he didn't think she would stick around.

As the elevator ascended the building's floors, Antonio closed his eyes. He pictured Paige and Christian. He smiled a little bit. They were his life. He had been slipping and losing sight lately, but he planned to make it up to them. As soon as he made this connection, he would make it up to them. Antonio was planning out how he'd wrap Paige up in his arms and tell her they didn't have any more financial worries, and how Christian would try to get in on the action with his sweet little hugs and affectionate nature.

When the elevator doors dinged open on the 50th floor, the penthouse, Jackson rushed out first. Another notable difference between Antonio and Jackson. This one Antonio couldn't let slide.

"Emil told us not to be too eager," Antonio mumbled disdainfully, glaring at Jackson. It was the first words they'd exchanged since they'd left the Bronx.

"Yo, nigga. What you not gonna do is tell me how to act in meetings that I've been going to years before your ass was on the scene," Jackson replied with a hateful snarl.

He couldn't even pretend to be happy about this arrangement if he wanted to. He was sour as hell that his father chose Antonio to lead this, or even be involved in the first place, rather than giving him free rein to take care of things. Especially because Emil had been really particular about keeping his connects to himself, something Jackson always resented. His father was a control freak, but all of a sudden, out of nowhere he was allowing an outsider into his deepest business. None of it made sense. Jackson knew that his father was a calculating man, so there had to be some kind of reason behind all of this. Still, he wasn't happy about the shit and felt slighted that his father didn't care to let him in on the plot.

Four young dudes stood like sentries in the hallway, awaiting their arrival. They looked like they still had fresh Similac on their breaths. Antonio's heart throttled up in his chest. One thing he did know from growing up in the rough streets of the Bronx was that young dudes were wild because they had little to nothing to live for.

The first dude, who resembled a baby-faced Lebron James, put his hand up, halting their movement. Another smaller, but screw-face youngin', waved Antonio forward. He rubbed his hands up and down the outside of Antonio's clothes. He guessed they were making sure he wasn't carrying no heat. They'd left their burners in the truck . . . another fact that had unnerved Antonio a little bit.

The men gave Jackson an even more thorough once over. They ran their hands along the legs of his jeans, around his ankles, and even between his legs. They made him remove his jewelry and even lift up his shirt to show that no wires were taped to his chest. These little boys weren't playing.

Once the pat-downs were complete, two more ruthless looking young dudes led them inside. Antonio's stomach did back flips as he stepped into the ultra-modern suite. The strong smell of weed immediately assailed his nose. He forced himself to swallow the bit of acidic vomit that had crept up his esophagus.

Jackson was acting like it was nothing—like he'd been to a thousand of these types of nerve-wracking meetings and he was too cool. Antonio knew better. He'd long ago figured out that Jackson was a lot of tough talk. Antonio wasn't so sure about how much action Jackson had in him.

The first thing that came to mind as Antonio looked around, was who the fuck was this guy? The penthouse was simply fucking breathtaking. The floor-to-ceiling glass windows rendered a breathtaking view of New York. Antonio felt like he was sitting on top of the world looking out those windows. Everything else inside was decorated red, white, and black. The walls were painted an institutional shade of white, and the marble-tiled floors looked fresh like purely fallen snow. There were four leather couches—two black, two red—circling a white leather ottoman that served as a coffee table in the center of the room. There were three white and red shaggy throw rugs that looked like no one had ever stepped on them either. To the left was a glass-top bar, the bottom tiled in white. Four eggcup, shiny red lacquer stools stood in front of the bar. Antonio felt slightly jealous. Here he had worked hard in the NBA for years and couldn't live like this. He wondered if he was going to make enough money to show Paige a life like this again.

Who would've ever thought a nobody like him would be sitting in a high-priced suite like this waiting to negotiate terms of a lucrative business deal? Antonio definitely was proud of himself.

"Yo, what up?" a voice echoed in the middle of the room. Antonio whirled around so fast he nearly stumbled backward. Jackson, with a scowl on his face, turned slowly like a gunslinger from the old Western movies. Neither Antonio nor Jackson was prepared for who they were seeing in front of them.

You gotta be fucking kidding me. Antonio blinked a few times to make sure his eyes weren't playing tricks on him. From his peripheral, he could see Jackson was thinking along the same lines. *What the fuck? Who the fuck?*

"So, I heard you the lost son," the man, well . . . boy, said out as he circled Antonio slowly. He literally looked like a little ass boy. He couldn't be any more than an even five feet tall. His face had no hair, not even peach fuzz. Talk about baby face criminal. The kid was flanked by three huge, wild-eyed young dudes that had no problem showing their guns to Antonio and Jackson.

"Nah, I'm the son. Jackson," Jackson stepped forward. The kid didn't flinch. He kept his eye on Antonio, who still wore an expression that said he couldn't believe that this little boy reaching out to shake his hand was the big bad connect that had all the so-called gangsters in New York running scared.

"Yeah, Jackson is Emil's son. I'm the associate," Antonio said. "And you are?" Antonio extended his hand for a shake.

"Everybody calls me Mo," the boy said. His baby face and barely deepened voice were actually making Antonio want to laugh. Mo looked like an escapee from a foster home rather than a deadly, billionaire drug kingpin.

"A'ight Mo," Antonio replied, trying to keep himself from staring too much or giggling. Mo reached out a little boy's hand. Antonio shook it firmly, and the boy seemed surprised at the grip.

"And you?" Mo said flatly to Jackson, eyeing him like he already didn't like him.

"Like I said before, I'm Jax," he said like he was offended that the little boy tried to play him like a nobody. "My pops ain't the only one making waves out here, so I'm sure if you heard of him, you heard of me," Jackson spat.

Antonio let out a long breath. He knew Jackson was stupid, but now he realized he was more like a fucking idiot.

"Nah, nigga, I ain't never heard of you," Mo said. "So you ain't all that, B."

Jackson went to open his mouth, but Antonio stepped between him and Mo.

"Let's get to it," Antonio said, his voice quivering.

"Yeah, how 'bout that," Mo said, still grilling Jackson. He moved over to his pristine couches. "Have a seat."

Antonio didn't feel comfortable but followed anyway. He sat on the very edge, back straight. Jackson sat next to him, also on the edge of his seat.

"First off, let me let y'all niggas know . . . I don't take no off-the-cuff meetings like this, especially not at my crib," Mo said, taking a freshly rolled blunt from one of his young guns. He took a long pull on his blunt. "But, I respect Emil Cartwright, and because I hate that motherfucker Max King, I agreed," Mo said, his voice sounding like he was struggling to breathe.

Antonio looked over at Jackson with a raised brow. Jackson shifted uncomfortably on the seat, causing the leather on the couch to crackle.

"Nah. We ain't gon' talk about King today," Jackson said, rushing his words out like the topic was forbidden. "This is all good business."

Antonio had heard the name Max King before, but it wasn't from Jackson, Hayden, or Emil. He scoured his mind, but in that moment, he was drawing a blank on the name. Antonio cleared his throat and put his hands up.

"Listen, I'm sure you're a busy ki—I mean dude. We appreciate the meeting. Understand, your enemies are our enemies," he assured.

The mood in the room shifted to uneasiness. Mo nodded at Antonio and blew out a thick stream of weed smoke. He seemed to be pondering what Antonio said.

"So, I hear you will be taking over this side of shit for Cartwright?" Mo asked and told at the same time, looking directly at Antonio.

Suddenly, it felt hot inside. This was the moment of truth.

"Well, not exactly. Jackson is going to take over with me, but Emil wanted a second chair on this deal," Antonio corrected, feeling the heat of Jackson's gaze on the side of his face. It wasn't what Emil wanted, but it was what Antonio, Jackson, and Hayden had agreed upon at the Blu. It was Antonio's way of treading lightly, for now.

The air in the room suddenly felt stifling. Tension buzzed like a swarm of bees around their heads.

"I guess you could say I would be in training, while Jackson runs things," Antonio clarified. Mo was suddenly seized by an uncontrollable rattling cough. It was like a combination of the weed and Antonio's words had choked him up. Antonio's eyes went wide. He looked at Jackson, who didn't seem to care or notice.

"Shit," Mo finally rasped as one of his young guns handed him a glass of water. His hands shook violently as he raised the glass to his lips. He sipped the water and handed it back to the boy. "A'ight. I'm good, now. So, you saying this hothead right here is going to run the shit but you just around for support?" Mo summarized for clarification.

Of course Jackson started to move, and Antonio had to put his hand on him. Mo's sarcastic tone was blowing Antonio's high. He wanted to jump up and slap this little kid, but he kept his cool. The little dude knew he could play tough, so he did. Period.

"We both will be working with you. That simple," Antonio replied, slightly annoyed. "I really don't have any experience with all of this. Emil wanted to have more than one of us in the know. It's what Emil wants. I will give Jax the lead, I just want to stay connected too, for my father's interest," Antonio explained.

"Nah," Mo said flatly.

Antonio raised his eyebrows. He felt like Mo had just spit in his face.

"In this business, the niggas on the street don't make the decision of who deals with the connect. The connect makes the decision on who the fuck I want to deal with," Mo chastised.

"Yo, you got a lot of mouth—" Jackson tried to interject. Antonio forcefully grabbed his arm. Mo's young guns moved closer to the scene based on Jackson's tone of voice.

"No offense intended," Antonio placated.

"Yeah, you better control your hot head brother, B," Mo said, sneering at Jackson.

"Now, I will not deal with anyone but you," Mo said, knowing he was dissing Jackson in his face and there wasn't shit he could do about it.

Jackson breathed out loudly and clenched his fists. The vein in his temple began beating fiercely against his skin. Antonio swallowed hard and shifted uncomfortably. He wasn't there to step on Jackson's toes, but there was really no way around it. *Shit!*

"What's your name again?" Mo asked Antonio.

"Tony. You can call me Tony."

"A'ight, Tony. Since it seems like you don't know, in this business there can only be one boss. Understand? If your father is the boss and I'm the connect, then that makes y'all the flunkies," Mo said.

Antonio looked on, growing more annoyed by the minute.

"So y'all niggas can fight amongst yourselves, but today, I chose to deal with you and not that lame nigga," Mo said, pointing at Jackson.

Jackson sprang up like a jack-in-the-box. This was not how he'd envisioned things going. He was clearly the next in line for the position since he was his father's oldest son. He was supposed to be the next Cartwright to take over shit.

"You think you know my family? He's not even at the amateur level in this game. Someone with no experience can really make this dangerous for all of our people," Jackson protested. His insides burned, his fists curled.

Mo's eager and waiting young dudes moved closer, but Mo didn't even react to Jackson's outburst. Jackson was outnumbered for sure. His eyes danced around the room. *Fuck!* He screamed in his head. If he wanted to make it out of there in one piece, he had to dial it down first. He wasn't stupid. Jackson's shoulders slumped in defeat, and he returned to his seat.

Mo seemed amused as he waited for him to finish making a fool of himself. Jackson hadn't swayed the kid one bit.

"Shit, everybody gotta learn. You ain't got no choice but to teach him what he needs to know, or you will be out of the business, and your father won't be fucking happy," Mo said dismissively, raising his hand. "Now, it's clear who I plan to deal with from now on. And, one more thing. Now that I've agreed to take y'all on, Max King will be coming down on y'all hard. That nigga hates me, and I hate him. He's like a tick on my ass. Just let Emil know that I warned y'all. This war requires all forces of whatever army y'all got. I don't make many partnerships either, so consider ya'selves fucking lucky," Mo said with deadly intent. He balled his fist and held it out in front of Antonio.

Antonio looked down at the little fist and wondered just how many men and women this little punk ass kid had killed with those hands. He shivered just thinking about what a kid like this might do to someone who crossed him. He was definitely a bold little dude.

"You got my word that your enemies are our enemies. We look forward to this business arrangement," Antonio assured while Jackson looked on, brooding.

"The cost of the next shipment is two million. I will take it in cash, or you can adjust prices of the next consignment to make up for it. Either way you choose to do it, I don't care. Just know that I need to be paid on time. That is how this business works."

Before he hobbled off, Mo turned his sights to Jackson.

"Teach him good and do right by him. Maybe one day, you'll even be able to earn my trust."

It was eerily silent on the way back to Jackson's car. Jackson sucked in his bottom lip and shoved his hands deep into the pockets of his pants like a kid who'd lost his favorite toy to his brother. It was all he could do to keep himself from putting his hands around Antonio's neck and squeezing until he passed out, or getting his gun and ending Antonio's threat to his position in the family.

Antonio knew his survival in this new endeavor depended fully on Jackson's mentoring. He had to keep the lines of communication between himself and Jackson open. Admittedly, Antonio didn't know the first thing about drug shipments—kilos versus bricks, consignment, distribution and percentages. . . . He needed to get humble quick, or he'd be in big trouble. He was good at putting himself in a means-to-an-end mindset, and right now, Jackson was his means-to-an-end. Swallowing hard and putting his usually stubborn pride aside, Antonio reached out and touched his brother's arm. Jackson bladed his body toward Antonio, his fists clenched and ready. Antonio snatched his hand away and put both hands up, a peace offering.

"C'mon, Jax. You know I have respect for you, man. I didn't expect things to go like that. Hell, I didn't expect

Emil to even put me in this position so fast. I had no control over how that little kid acted and how he wanted to proceed with business. Trust me, I'm not into stepping on toes. I'm here to learn, to grow. I need you now just as much as you need me. You have my word. I'm not trying to take your place, man. I just want to get in where I fit in and for all of us to eat," Antonio said in his sincerest voice.

Jackson contemplated his brother's little spiel. His jaw loosened, and his eyes softened a little bit. He wanted to scream and curse about his father. This wasn't the first time Emil had slighted him for someone else. For Jackson, it was like his father was constantly subliminally telling him that he wasn't proud of him. But, in that moment, father's wishes or not, Jackson knew he held all the cards, because if he told Antonio to fuck off, they'd all be screwed—including that little bastard, Mo. Jackson also knew that he would be screwed too, which made his decision to go along with the plan a bit easier. He loved the fast life too much. The money, the women, the popularity . . . he was addicted to it all in a dangerous way.

"Whatever, nigga," Jackson said, lightening up. "Just don't ever say I didn't warn you before you jumped off the side of the building into this shark tank. It ain't no place for a soft-ass ball-playing nigga like you. Once you're in, you can't ever get out, unless you go out the way a lot of soldiers do . . . the grave," Jackson said ominously. Then he stalked toward the building's exit. Antonio bit the inside of his cheek and followed closely behind. It was too late to think about it now. He was already all in.

Once inside the car, Antonio reached down and turned Jackson's music off. Jackson's eyebrows shot up into arches.

"Nigga, you—" Jackson started.

Antonio cut him off. "You know, it's been over two months since I started working with y'all, and we've never really gotten a chance to know one another. Me and you. Brothers. Man to man. We will be stuck together like glue now, so I think now is that time," Antonio said. He meant it, but he also needed to get Jackson to reveal things Antonio would never get from Emil and Hayden. Jackson may have been a loose cannon, but Antonio had sensed that he was the most honest of the three. There was still something missing from the stories Emil shared, and Antonio had a feeling that Jackson had the answers.

Jackson rubbed his chin as he contemplated Antonio's request. A part of him didn't want to share anything with this outsider. His life was his business. Another part of him wanted Antonio to know who Emil Cartwright really was, since Antonio seemed to believe their father was this great man and not a ruthless drug kingpin hiding behind legitimate businesses. With one hand on the steering wheel, Jackson thought about it all.

"When we started in the business, I was eighteen and Hayden was just sixteen. Pop had always provided a nice life for us. He was already established as the man in every business he touched . . . legal and illegal. Pop didn't believe in sending us to the white man's schools. He schooled us at home. Back then, my moms wasn't feeling that shit. She used to preach to Pop about how our customers were our own people—somebody's mother or somebody's deadbeat-ass father. Pop sold to our own with no qualms about it. Pop looked at it like this: he had started out from the gate trying to make his life better. Back in his day, nobody was giving him shit. He had to scrap and struggle to move up. He told us stories about when his family came up north from the South and he was so broke he couldn't afford simple shit like a haircut, clean clothes, or shoes with soles in them. Pop said his mother used to work for them white people cleaning until her hands bled. He got tired of watching that shit, so he started hanging around the cats back then that had the Cadillac cars and the tailor-made suits," Jackson looked over at Antonio. "Most of them niggas was pimps, and Pop said he had too much respect for his mother to make a woman sell pussy for his come up. He started in the dope business instead."

"Just like that? It was that easy back then?" Antonio questioned, truly intrigued to be learning his father's back story.

"Pop was unique," he replied. "Nobody could even hold a match to Pop in certain areas. He was smart—real book smart and street smart. Some of the dudes he came up in the game with couldn't even do basic math or read and write, but Pop had taught himself. The other guys were getting robbed blind by their suppliers. Pop had survival skills. He was always explaining stuff to dudes on the street, real analytical-like. Pop read a lot of books, even them boring ass textbooks. As he got older, Pop learned to play the middle so well that he was able to have the best of both worlds. He could mix in with them white folks and talk all proper and shit, but he told us he would come home and hang on the block with the cats that wasn't fuckin' with the white man's world. Pop was smarter than all them niggas back then—black or white. He knew the keys to the game were in knowing how to expertly play the game," Jackson continued.

Antonio understood that all too well. He'd had his fair share of having to play the game to navigate life. Like now—he didn't really want to be a part of the Cartwright family, in fact, he hated that they had everything he never did, but his mastery of game-playing had gotten him this far, and he had no other options left to provide for his wife and child.

"I knew he was smart," Antonio placated so he could hear more.

"Smart? Nah, that nigga was a genius. Did you know that he was so genius, he played himself down? The nigga was already nearly a millionaire from the streets, but he wasn't satisfied with that. He knew shit could be bigger and better. Pop became a custodian in them tall, shiny, white people business buildings in Manhattan and he caught on that most of them rich working people were addicts. The dude started selling to them, and he would make a grip daily just off two or three of his white customers. As we got older, Pop would tell us the only difference between us and them was they had way more money to spend, which also meant we had way more money to make. He was making his paper daily, round the clock, and those white motherfuckers ain't even have to leave their desks. Pop was hitting them off with that eighty percent pure white at the time. It was top-of-the-line shit. Pop told us how word of mouth about him spread all over Manhattan like a fucking plague. Them white boys loved him. He charged top dollar, and for the convenience of having their dealer deliver, they paid whatever he asked. If they ain't have the money, Pop made deals. Big deals. But you know, as with anything, deals, money . . . that shit breeds jealousy and envy."

"So how did he get a hold of the blow to begin with? Who was his supplier?" Antonio asked, intrigued by this other side of Emil.

"That's what made Pop so powerful in the streets. The mystery behind him. He never talked about where he got his product from and we never asked. When he was making his money in Manhattan, he eventually caught on that moving up to the Bronx would make his money even longer. So that's what he did. As we got older, he showed us the ropes. But you know he always preached about wanting more. He would have me distribute to his street-level niggas. His product was so good that it only took a little to make what they were putting out there. Even if them niggas broke it all the way down, people loved the shit. Everybody was happy." Jackson said, smirking like he was off in some far away fairytale land that didn't exist anymore.

"Was he happy then?" Antonio pressed.

"After a few years, we learned that this old head, Max King, wasn't feeling Pop moving in on his territory. Pop was fearless, and he even moved in on Max's legal shit. Pop was washing his dirty money and found out one of his clients had invested it in some stocks. Pop wanted to build his own shit. He used to work in the business buildings, and he moved up to owning them shits. Me? I was a boss in my own right. Pop told me it was a mistake to trust those young kids to work for me, but I told him I could handle myself. I told him let square ass Hayden run the legit shit and let me stick to this street. I don't know, shit just kind of changed for me and Pop along the way. It's like he wanted me to be something I'm not—a square nigga. He kind of dissed me a few times over the years," Jackson's voice was full of regret. His mood swung like a pendulum from happy, to sad, to angry as he recalled the past.

"If it makes you feel better, he's always said you were smart . . . real street smart," Antonio said, almost feeling sorry for Jackson.

"I can admit, I am stubborn, and sometimes I didn't follow his advice. That shit led me to the system, and if it wasn't for Pop, his clean money, and them lawyers, I wouldn't be sitting here talking to your ass today. That's facts."

"One of Pop's first legitimate businesses was a bar called Ladies and Gents, right in the heart of the hood.

It was like a 'fuck you' to the Feds and the police that had been tracking Pop's every move. He was like Bumpy Johnson, the urban Robin Hood and shit. The first night of business, everybody ate and drank for free. I thought that nigga was crazy. It hurt my heart to see how much money Pop was letting slip through his fingers. But that method in the hood worked like a fucking charm. From that day forward, Pop had loyal customers and lookouts and protectors. The place was always packed, even on the nights when there was fucking snowstorms and shit.

"That same month, things went to shit for me. I got caught up in a sweep on the street. Even though I had eased off the hand-to-hand sales, I had a few kids still working for me. Just like Pop had warned me against. Life had been good for me up to that point. I was out from Pop's shadow, but that also meant I was out from under the cover of his protection. All it took was one worker to get knocked. That snitch nigga told the cops all about me pushing weight, about the re-up spots, and about the blocks I had my people holding down. Thanks to that nigga, I ended up walking right into a narco trap. Pop never visited me, but he sent a top-notch team of lawyers to work on my case. I was on the inside going crazy, thinking that Pop and Hayden had turned their backs on me until them fucking lawyers showed up, sharp as shit and ready to get me out of there. I can appreciate that shit now. Pop was smarter than me. An old head that knew better. He wouldn't dare bring heat to himself by visiting me. Too many eyes on him, enemies and cops alike. Trust me, to this day and always, Pop thinks all of his actions through. He was never a fly-by-the-seat-of-ya-pants type of dude," Jackson said, his head rocking in earnest.

Antonio shook his head in agreement. Learning this fact about Emil made him slightly uncomfortable, because Emil's decision to thrust him into this business seemed to be a knee-jerk decision. Why would he all of a sudden be making quick decisions? That question nagged Antonio. His thoughts were broken up by Jackson's voice.

"I wasn't behind bars for longer than a hot minute. I got off. My dream team of lawyers fried that fucking snitch on the stand. By the time they finished, his credibility was like a pile of horse shit," Jackson chuckled.

"Then what?" Antonio asked.

"Then I came home. Ready to work. Pop was different toward me after that, though. He wasn't the same toward me ever," Jackson said, his voice going low.

Antonio couldn't figure out if he was sad or mad at the revelation that his father changed toward him.

"I found out later too that Pop was stressed because he'd gotten word that your moms was dying," Jackson blurted.

Antonio's heart immediately throttled up in his chest. He whipped his head to the side and stared at side of Jackson's face. Antonio's breath came out in jagged puffs.

"The one thing Pops didn't do was lie to us. He married my mother, but he told us point blank, he was in love with yours. I'm talking like, he was with our mother for years and never stopped professing his love for your mother."

Antonio cleared his throat. It was all he could do to keep from cursing and screaming, *If he loved her so fucking much why did he leave her broken-hearted to struggle? Why did he leave us to struggle?*

"For a dude like Pop who could buy his way out of every situation, it was real hard to stand by totally powerless. And on top of that, our mother wanted out of the marriage. She had had enough of playing second fiddle to Pop's real love. He was doing good in business, but his personal life was falling apart. Pop ain't want nobody to show him no sympathy. He wanted to roll solo. His businesses kind of suffered, but he didn't care. We were all mad at him, but he didn't care. All the years growing up, I had never seen him show no real emotions, but he cried like a baby the day your moms passed. He just wanted to be left alone. Pop disappeared for about a year after your moms closed her eyes. But before he left, he made sure he told us about you," Jackson said, following up with a long sigh.

Antonio was speechless. What was he supposed to say to that? He wanted to change the subject. He didn't want to hear any more about his mother and her pain. He had lived it. He had worked years to bury that painful experience.

"Back to the business . . . Emil disappeared, and then what?" Antonio pressed. He just wanted to get off the topic of his mother.

"In the year Pop took off from the business, shit had changed drastically. There was a whole new system out on the blocks that used to be mine. It was like some underground sales shit—no more standing outside, hoodies on, stashing your shit in a brown paper bag, hand-to-hand transactions. Nah, there was an elaborate code of cash exchange and transfer system. Nobody was allowed to speak on the phone about anything at all. It was all official, roundtable meetings and shit. That's when I met all of the distributors, and everybody wanted to become like the mafia. They were working the new system like pros. It had all been set up by Pop, but I didn't even know. They respected him like he was the next messiah. Yeah, to this day, even with his shortcomings, Pop is the fucking smartest businessman in town. He turned corner sales into a well-oiled business machine. Even the fiends knew how shit worked, and they respected it," Jackson recalled, his tone changing again.

"So where did that leave you?" Antonio asked the obvious question.

"For a while, that left me nowhere. Pop never left me hungry—that's a fact. He made sure I still had finest clothes, jewelry, a spot to lay my head and shit. I would never take that away from him. But, when you grow up in the game, somebody taking your shit over, even your own father, is like taking the air out of your lungs and holding a gun to your head to force you to breathe.

"When Pop got over your mother's death, he came back on the scene and we had a big blow up about my role in the business. I told him how fucked up I felt about him snatching up my business. But, you know his style. he is a smooth-talking old motherfucker that could shut you down with your own words. He told me he had bigger plans for me and Hayden. Told me, I was better than that penny street corner business. Pop convinced me that he wanted me to be his right hand, a position that would make me a lot more money and gain me a lot of respect.

"I was hesitant at first. I ain't want to be no square. Wearing a suit and shit ain't my thing," Jackson said, raising an eyebrow and looking over at Antonio's suit. "Pop assured me that he would never lead me wrong. For the first time in my life he told me he loved me. I was twenty-fucking-one years old before my own father ever told me he loved me. I felt that shit, too. From that day forward, I did whatever Pop asked of me. I would've followed him into the pits of Hell if he asked me. I was loyal. Loyal like a dog. But, you know, as with everything, all good things get fucked up when other shit come into the mix," Jackson said, his emotions raw.

Antonio sensed he was still holding something back. Some hurt between him and Emil that was still too painful to talk about. Antonio was confused. Shit, what was the problem? Jackson had the love of his father, something Antonio never had. If Emil had made Jackson his right-hand man, why was he still not all the way cool?

"Pop, on some levels, is generous, smart, and rich, but he is also egotistical, mean, and sometimes straight-up cruel," Jackson clarified.

Antonio tilted his head, curious, his eyebrows arched on his face.

"How long was I supposed to stay just doing his dirty work? It ain't take me long to figure out that Pop didn't want a partner like he said, he wanted a slave. He wanted to make me believe I was important, but he was using me. That shit was real obvious, too. He was secretive and told me what he wanted me to know . . . just enough that I couldn't really be on my own out here. I mean, I was selling keys to bosses from up in the Bronx all the way down to far-ass places on South Carolina, and I never knew exactly what cut Pop was getting off that. I mean, he paid me, but four or five stacks out of a duffle bag full seemed like nothing to me when I thought about him taking the entire bag, minus the pennies he threw to me. I always wanted more. I wanted in deeper. I wanted to walk by his side, not follow like some slave bitch behind him. I wanted to help make business decisions, not take instructions all the time. Pop never even introduced me to his connects. I found out about them through word of mouth on the streets.

"After I confronted Pop about always being left out of the loop, he pacified me a little bit. He told me about his first connect and the Piña Cartel from Mexico, but never took me to the meetings he had with them. I should've been more than a worker by then, especially after we got our own legitimate businesses. That shit was lost on Hayden, who was just happy to think that we all owned the legitimate businesses, but it wasn't lost on me. We don't own those shits—Pop owns them. He had his high-priced lawyers make sure of that. Cartwright Enterprises my ass. Do you think I own a real interest in the business?

I always knew the deal. I knew Pop's intentions when he fronted those legitimate businesses. It damn sure wasn't for the reason he said—so we could all eventually walk away from the drug game.

"It's like this, a hungry motherfucker who gets hungry enough gonna take food from anybody, even the bastard who starved him in the first place. Pop starved us and then fed us when he was ready, like them terrorists do when they capture hostages. His own fucking kids. If a dude showed that he was too smart for Pop, that dude would either be out immediately, or he would disappear, never to be heard from again. You think it would be different for us? So, I learned how to play my role, but deep inside, I ain't happy about this.

"As time went on, Pop started expanding his whole-sale business. He opened the imports business and the Mexicans were shipping the shit in by the boatload. That shit came in paintings, food, toys, car rims, car engines . . . anything. I never knew cocaine could be liq-uefied and turned into so many things. Pop even had them cops at the New York Harbor Police in his pocket. The mayor was on payroll, and so was the police com-missioner. His shit was airtight. Truth be told, I was the one taking the risk because I worked the shipments. I was out there at four in the morning when shit arrived. I was the one in warehouses risking my life and free-dom to distribute across the city. Those bosses could've murked me, took the goods, and kept their money at any time during those meets. My job was worth more than I was getting paid from my own father, and so I asked to be made equal. Pop flatly said no to my request. I ques-tioned that, and he went off. He got in my face, telling me to fucking remember where I came from—that he was my father and he had made me. That shit hurt me, like my own father had stabbed me in the heart. I was mentally on some destructive shit after that," Jackson gritted with contempt.

Antonio's eyes were round as he watched a whirlwind of emotions play out in Jackson's facial expressions.

Jackson looked over at Antonio as they pulled up to their business building.

"Why you looking at me like that?" Jackson asked. "What, you thought your father was some angel? Pshh, far from it nigga."

Antonio shook his head. His hands shook. Something about Jackson's words sent a chill through him.

"C'mon, I'm just talking nigga. I love my Pops. I said I *was* on some destructive shit. That don't mean I really want to destroy shit. I would've never done anything like that to Pop . . . that's my word," he assured. "After all, the nigga did give me life."

Antonio wasn't so convinced that Jackson wasn't out to destroy his own father. Something in Antonio's gut was telling him that none of the Cartwrights should be trusted. He'd heard enough. His nerves were frazzled now.

"When can we meet to go over things? Mo's people will be contacting me soon." Antonio quickly changed the subject.

"Oh, it's like that. No more discussing Pop?" Jackson replied, chuckling evilly. He knew he'd said too much. That was part of his plan.

"Look, I'm sorry for everything you went through, bro. Right now, we are all at his mercy. He may not, but I see you as one above me. I'm new to this in some ways, so that automatically puts you on a higher level in game," Antonio placated, the lies rolling off his tongue freely. He didn't see Jackson as one above him whatsoever. They were all Emil's sons, and like it or not, he was going to get what was owed to him.

"Whatever, man. We can meet tomorrow. We always meet at the Blu," Jackson told him.

Antonio nodded. He stuck out his fist for a pound. Then he exited Jackson's truck. He could feel the heat of Jackson's gaze on his back as he walked into the Cartwright Enterprises building. Both of them were probably thinking the same thing: *this nigga needs me just as much as I need him.*

Chapter 8

All Falls Down

Paige had a headache. A massive, temple-pulsing, eye-blinding headache. She sat up painfully straight, trying to act like she was okay. But she couldn't help that her eyes darted to the door of the venue no less than every five minutes since she'd been there. The five minutes before were the same as the five minutes after. Nothing. Her mother flitted around the place and then back to the table several times, but each time, Paige ignored her. Lillian was always talking, and tonight, Paige just couldn't listen. Paige picked up her glass of sparkling water and took a sip. If her Antonio didn't show up soon, Paige knew she'd be having more than sparkling water.

"Are you alright? You look stunning as usual, but your mind is clearly off to another place," Lillian said, sitting down next to Paige.

"Thanks, Mother. I've already told you, I have a slight headache. But, I'm here, smiling through it. I learned from the best," Paige said, flashing another phony smile, realizing her mother was trying to make small talk to avoid the awkwardness of Antonio's absence.

"Look who just had the fucking nerve to arrive," a friend at the table said, looking past Paige's shoulder.

Paige turned her head slightly and then back to her mother, incredulous.

"Lori Standley," Lillian whispered. "The new bitch sleeping with your father."

Paige blanched. "What?" she rasped. She eyed the olive-skinned beauty who'd sauntered into the venue like she owned it. The woman's perfectly beat makeup, her cascading dark, bone-straight hair, and her beautiful shape were hard to miss.

Paige looked toward the door again, hoping Antonio was going to be next to walk in, but again, nothing. She inhaled deeply and exhaled.

"I don't think she's Daddy's type," Paige said, blinking a few times before she turned her attention back to her mother.

"You're wrong. I know for a fact. But, it's okay. I have something for your father this time. I just chose to stay quiet for now," Lillian said with a forced cheerfulness in her tone that actually scared Paige.

"Now, where is that husband of yours? You know your father expects him to be here every year, and this year is no different."

Paige sighed and hung her head. She was tired of making excuses now. Antonio had missed quite a few events. If anyone knew what Paige was going through in that moment, it was her mother. After all, Lillian was the wife of a very busy man. Truth be told, Gladstone Tillary was absent from his family more than he was present. Paige had watched her mother field her fair share of absent husband questions when Paige was a child. She had always seen her mother do it, wearing the kind of smile she was wearing now. Phony. Forced. Pretend.

"Ahh, look who's here," Lillian chimed and waved. "Your bestie."

Paige looked up just in time to see Michaela waltzing in.

"Oh, and how ironic, right behind her is your husband," Lillian said snidely, raising a brow at Paige but still smiling and waving to Michaela.

"What's that supposed to mean?"

"I just never trusted her," Lillian grunted.

Paige looked at her watch again and noted that Antonio was over two hours late. Her father approached and grunted from behind her. Paige whirled around and smiled at her father. She could see the flicker of judgment and suspicion glinting in his eyes. She had spent her entire life making sure that in Gladstone's eyes, she was always daddy's perfect little girl.

"So, where is your husband?" her father asked brusquely.

"He just arrived," Paige replied, nodding toward the other side of the room where Antonio and Michaela were together, smiling and speaking to folks as they made their way around the massive room. From afar, people might've mistaken Michaela for Antonio's wife. Something about it caused Paige's headache to intensify. It was something that had bothered her for years. Michaela had always been far too friendly with Antonio.

"He is over two hours late. What? He has no respect for you. And then he walks around like he's the politician here?"

Paige sighed. No matter how many years had passed and no matter what Antonio did, her parents were always going to find fault with him. They hated him, and they couldn't even hide it.

Paige understood that her father was old school. In their family, respect, reputation, and keeping your word meant everything. When he allowed Antonio to marry his only daughter, Gladstone had made it clear that Paige was to be treated like a precious gem. Gladstone never gave Antonio a break. He believed real men made their money through hard work, not playing basketball. It didn't matter to Gladstone that Antonio had at one time signed a lucrative multi-million-dollar contract.

"He needs to get his shit together for once in his life," Gladstone said sharply.

Paige balked at her father's verbal slap. There were so many things she wanted to say to her father in that moment, but, as usual, Paige backed down when it came to him.

Paige rolled her eyes and let out an exasperated breath. Although her appearance was perfect, her life was far from it. Paige had spent years pretending that she and Antonio had the perfect marriage. The truth was, she had become an expert at ignoring what she didn't want to see. Like her best friend and her husband arriving at the same time, both late.

"Oh, here he is now," Paige beamed, her shoulders drooping with relief. Paige was raging inside, but still she smiled. The look Antonio wore on his face was like a kid who'd missed his curfew—arched eyebrows, wide-stretched eyes, and a fake, toothy grin. Guilty.

"Sorry I'm late. Last minute meeting," Antonio said, too smoothly and too calmly for Paige's liking. He knew she was seething, because he totally avoided eye contact with her.

Paige tapped her foot on the floor under the table. Unconsciously, her eyes hooded over and her lips flattened into a straight line. Watching Antonio walk to the table didn't give Paige the warm and tingly feeling she'd experienced in the beginning of their relationship. All she could see was the pain and agony of staying married to him. Paige told herself in that moment that she'd had enough. She wanted a divorce. Just thinking about it made her stomach swirl.

"Mr. T," Antonio said cheerfully, extending his hand toward Paige's father for a handshake. "As usual you have a good turnout for your campaign event." Antonio was laying it on thick, and everyone in earshot knew it.

Gladstone knew how his son-in-law felt about him, and the feelings were definitely mutual. Both men played the game for Paige.

Gladstone grunted and reluctantly took Antonio's hand. Gladstone squeezed a little harder than a normal handshake allowed. Paige noticed, and a warm sense of satisfaction burst in her chest when she saw Antonio wince slightly.

"Lillian," Antonio sang, awkwardly wrestling his hand away from his father-in-law. "Looking young and beautiful as ever," he sang, kissing Lillian on the cheek. Lillian blushed, of course. Paige rolled her eyes. It didn't take much to sway her mother back to the other side.

When Antonio finally turned his attention to Paige, she smiled, but her insides were churning so hard it felt like her organs were going through a meat grinder. Antonio took a seat next to her and planted a dry kiss on her cheek. "You look amazing tonight. But, you always do. Always flawless," he said.

Paige swallowed the hard lump that had formed in her throat. The word *divorce* popped into her mind again.

"Ahem," Paige cleared her throat. "Now that you're here, I can make my toast," she said regarding Antonio coolly. Paige raised her glass and lowered her eyes toward the sparkling liquid inside. She had already caught sight of the dark, purple love bite peeking from Antonio's collar and the flushed look on Michaela's face. Michaela, who still hadn't come and greet her.

"Here's to my father, a great man with a great legacy. A real man who always puts his family first. A man of integrity and honesty. Here's to the man I know I can always rely on even when all others fail me," Paige said pointedly, looking at Antonio so hard she forced him to look away first.

***

Gladstone couldn't wait for a moment away from the women to confront Antonio. He walked up behind Antonio and cleared his throat. Antonio almost spilled his drink as he turned around to find his father-in-law standing uncomfortably close.

"I heard that you're working for your father now," Gladstone said, getting right to the point.

Antonio's face fell into a frown. "You heard correctly. I'm retired from basketball and didn't want to be left idle."

"That's funny. I didn't know you two had gotten close. Hell, I didn't know you talked. I mean, I thought I knew the story of how he'd left you and your mother to live in poverty while he lavished his other sons with riches," Gladstone said cruelly. While he took under-the-belt shots against Antonio, he would never tell him that he suspected, before his son-in-law even knew his father's name, that he was Emil's son.

Antonio chuckled. It was a predictable line of conversation. His father-in-law got off on making other people feel small. He was one of those people who needed the weakness of others to feel powerful.

"Well, part of that is true. My father and I hadn't talked much over the years. But, you know, there's always room for forgiveness. You know all about second chances, don't you?"

Gladstone's eyes lowered into slits. "Look. If you were having financial issues, you could've came to me. Emil Cartwright might be your biological father, but you're still married to my daughter. I don't know what you know about him, but he's far from Cliff Huxtable. And you know how seriously I take my reputation." They both knew that he was referencing that night, all those years ago, when they first entered one another's lives.

"With all due respect, Mr. Tillary, I know you might mean well, but I wouldn't come to you if my eyebrows were on fire and I needed someone to spit on them. Besides, come to you so you could judge me as unworthy, like you've been doing all these years? Emil is my father . . . and I know you're worried about your family name, but he's actually my family, so I don't give a shit about your worries."

"Listen, son," Gladstone whispered harshly, moving so close to Antonio's face he felt the heat of his breath on his lips. "Emil Cartwright is not who you think he is. I've seen him eat his own many times. So I hope, for your sake, he doesn't have you doing anything illegal. I'd hate for that to blow back on my daughter, and more importantly, just know I will not allow it to blow back on me and my family."

Antonio laughed, but it contradicted the fear thrumming inside of him. "Illegal? Of course not. I'm managing the family import and export business with my brothers. I know it may be hard to believe that anyone else can be as together as your family, but the Cartwrights are pretty damn close. And Emil built that family from scratch. He wasn't handed a family name to use to rise to the top like you," Antonio said, staring Gladstone directly in the eyes.

Gladstone picked up his whisky from the bar. He raised the glass and smirked. "Have it your way, son. Just watch yourself. You've done very well all these years without his help. I wouldn't want you to get rounded up in an investigation. Because trust me, it won't be long before Emil Cartwright is the subject of yet another investigation."

"I believe that all of that stuff is behind him. As far as I know, every single time you've tried to get him, you've failed. I don't think it'll be different the next time you try, or the time after that or after that," Antonio said, also raising his glass and smirking.

Gladstone's usually light, butter-colored skin was now a deep shade of red. His nostrils flared, but he kept his cool.

"I hope so. For your sake, I hope so," Gladstone growled under his breath. He didn't take defeat lightly.

Antonio patted Gladstone on the shoulder. "You don't have to hope." And with that, he walked away.

Gladstone downed his next drink and turned toward the crowd. The tension from the conversation still showed on his face. But, what he saw next, sent his dark mood into overdrive. He slammed his drink down and stormed toward Lori, who'd just walked into the arm of another man.

"This bitch," Gladstone mumbled as he headed straight for Lori and her date.

"Senator Tillary," Lori sang, seemingly grabbing her date's arm harder. "What a great turnout you have tonight." Lori was taunting Gladstone and she knew it.

Before he could make his unhappiness known, Lillian was standing there. Lillian hated to see Lori. She hated everything about her. Although Gladstone always swore that they only had a working relationship, and Lori was like a daughter, Lillian knew better. She had been with him long enough to know when he was fucking someone.

"Well, well, well," Lillian said snidely.

"Mrs. Tillary!" Lori said with phony excitement. "You look radiant tonight." Lillian squinted at Lori and then back at her husband. She could tell by his face that he was not happy to see his precious Lori with another man.

"You must think I'm stupid," Lillian snapped. Her bravado had come from all of the drinks she had been knocking down, back to back. "You're the only one in the dark, Senator," Lillian hissed, pushing Gladstone roughly in the chest.

Several guests turned toward the small commotion. Gladstone grabbed Lillian's hand and tried to pretend everything was fine.

"Unhand me! You don't want everyone to know about her," Lillian yelled, kicking her shoes off in Lori's direction.

Lori jumped back, shocked.

Gladstone tightened his grip on his drunk wife. "Lillian, I am not for this tonight. It's time for us to leave before you embarrass yourself any more than you already have," he said through clenched teeth.

"Me? Embarrass *me*? No. It's too late. You've already embarrassed me for years," Lillian boomed, her words slurring. "You allowed this bitch . . . your mistress . . . oh, wait . . . just *one* of your mistresses, to come to this event like it was okay? You think I don't know about them all? You've been exposed, Senator-fucking-Tillary," Lillian spat.

Loud gasps and groans erupted around the room. People pulled out cell phones and began recording. Security rushed around, trying to stop the disaster, but it was too late.

Lillian stormed out of the venue. She ran straight into Antonio, who was outside the venue talking to Jackson.

"Lillian? What's wrong?" Antonio asked.

"What do you care? All of you bastards are the same! You're making money with your crooked father now. You're carrying on with my daughter's friend too, huh?" Lillian barked.

"Mother!" Paige shouted.

Lillian and Antonio turned around, shocked to find Paige and Michaela standing there. Paige and Michaela had followed Lillian outside to check on her.

"Only you can't see it, Paige," Lillian slurred, not backing down from her point.

Paige reacted as if her mother had slapped her in the face. It was one thing for her mother to make comments like this in private, to talk through these things quietly, but in public? In front of both Antonio and Michaela? Her mother had stolen her rage. She turned toward Michaela. For the first time in their friendship, Michaela was speechless. Paige looked at Antonio, hurt glinting in her eyes.

He put his hands up. "Paige, listen," he started.

Paige knew him. She knew as soon as her name came out of this mouth followed by "listen," that he was about to lie.

"You. Piece. Of. Shit," Paige croaked out, her words coming out in rough waves of emotion. Her anger and rage, mixed with pain of years of having forgiven his tres-passes, flowed out. Tears immediately sprang to her eyes. She looked at Michaela. "And you. My oldest friend. You comforted me with his other bitches," Paige screamed. "I never thought you would do this. Never." She took off running, her sobs threatening to choke her to death.

"Paige, wait!" Antonio yelled after her.

Lillian was beyond embarrassed and drunk. All she wanted to do was get out of there by any means.

"Who are you?" she asked Jackson, stumbling toward him.

"I'm Jax, his brother," Jackson said, nodding in the direction that Antonio ran after Paige.

"Listen, I'm his mother-in-law. I'm rich, and I need to get the hell out of here. I'll pay you for a ride home. Please, I just need to go."

Jackson smirked. It was like he was watching a soap opera take place. "Sure. I'll give you a ride. No payment needed," he said. Of course he obliged, this was the per-fect way to work his way into the life of one of his father's greatest enemies.

***

As Michaela stood outside watching Antonio chase down Paige, she realized how right she was. She and Rod weren't going to get a divorce, because she had signed that stupid deal to be on Casey's dumb-ass show. Her outburst at his birthday party was enough to boost ratings for the next couple of months, and both of them were more about the money than about each other. Instead, they were going to stay married, and he was going to cheat on her, and she was going to let him, because she loved Louboutins and Balenciaga bags. She looked at Antonio as he hustled after her friend and she wondered if Rod would ever run after her like that. But she knew that he wouldn't.

Earlier that night, Michaela had made a terrible mistake. And really, she didn't even know how it had happened. She had driven herself to the fundraiser that night in her white Maserati Levante, Rod had gotten it for her as a present after they had signed to the show. The producers had eaten it up. But now she was parked in the lot, sitting behind the steering wheel trying not to cry and giving herself a pep talk.

"Okay, Michaela, you got this," she said into the pull-down mirror. Her red YSL lipstick caught the light of a car pulling in behind her. She groaned. There went all her privacy. She had her head down on the steering wheel when somebody knocked on her window. She jumped, hitting her head on the roof of the car, but before she could scream, she realized that it was just Antonio. Michaela laughed and rolled down the window.

"What are you doing out here?" asked Antonio, flashing that same smile he always gave her. She knew she wasn't special, that he smiled like that to everyone, but there had always been something about the way he talked to her that made her feel like she was the only person in the world.

"Oh, you know, I was just taking a little break before I went into that whole thing. What are you doing though? Why aren't you inside yet?" asked Michaela.

His smile faded away. He seemed nervous.

"I was just handling some business with my brothers. No big deal, really," he assured her, flashing that smile again. She started to tear up. "Wait, oh no, why are you crying?" asked Antonio. He looked around to see if anyone else was in the parking lot and then ran around the car and got in the passenger seat.

"It's just been hard ever since Rod and I, reached our . . . agreement, or whatever," she said, moving her hair out of her face, making sure her outburst hadn't ruined her look. She had spent time on her hair and makeup, because this was the first time she was leaving the house since everything had gone down.

"No, I get that," said Antonio. He was sitting squarely in the passenger seat. He didn't want anyone to pass by and think anything unsavory was happening, because it wasn't. "Marriage is something that you need to work on. No one is without their problems," he continued. He thought about him and Paige, and how hard things had been ever since he had lost all of their money in that ridiculous-ass scheme. He should take his own advice. Michaela laughed.

"You both have to want to work, though," she said quietly, her eyes on the Maserati logo in the middle of the steering wheel. She had not thought that she loved Rod enough to feel hurt like this. It was taking over her whole body. She thought that she could blame what happened next on having lost her heart somewhere along the way.

On his side of the car, Antonio could feel the energy change. He was worried that he had maybe said the wrong thing. He turned to look at Michaela, but she was already looking at him, tears pooling at the edges of her eyes. She put her hand on his thigh, unable to stop herself. Antonio had spent so many years loving Paige the way that people only get loved in fairytales—couldn't he love her too?

"Michaela, we can't do this," Antonio said, trying to edge away from her. He had no idea what had come over his wife's best friend.

"Please," she whispered, moving her hand higher up on his leg. Antonio winced, a mixture of pleasure and guilt. Taking her opportunity, while he was weak with shock, Michaela put her mouth on his neck, passionately kissing him. A little too passionately. Antonio gave into the pleasure for a few moments before snapped back to reality. He jumped, forcing her off of him.

"No, God, no," he yelled, "what is wrong with you?" His whole life flashed before his eyes. He had no idea where everything had gone so wrong so quickly. First, he had gotten cut from the team, and then he had lost all of their money and savings, and then he had got caught up with the Cartwrights, and now this? Paige's best friend in the whole world was trying to seduce him. It was too much. Paige could forgive a lot of things, but she couldn't forgive this

Michaela almost couldn't believe what she had just done. But a part of her also could. She had always had a sweet spot for Antonio, and even though she had never admitted it to Paige, or even herself, she was always so jealous of the fact he had set his eyes on Paige all those years ago and not her. As Antonio freaked out next to her, Michaela had to admit that a part of her had wanted him this whole time. She heard a slam as Antonio got out and began to walk toward the fundraiser. Quickly, she threw on her shoes and ran after him.

Now, as she stood outside, almost in the same place that she ran in after Antonio, Michaela thought about all the damage she had done. About all the hurt she had caused her friend. She would have said Rod too, but she truly didn't think that he loved her enough to care.

Chapter 9

Making Moves

Two weeks after the first meeting with Mo, Antonio sat next to Jackson in the backseat of the second of three heavily-tinted black Cadillac Escalades as they caravanned through the Bronx, resembling a presidential motorcade. The dark streets rapidly whipped by the SUV's windows. Antonio was still always amazed that at three o'clock in the morning, the hood was alive with people like it was noontime. It was business as usual, which meant he and the Cartwrights would always be in business.

"Nervous, nigga?" Jackson asked, breaking the unsettling quiet inside the car.

"Psh, c'mon. Only you think I'm soft. I know what's up," Antonio responded, lying. He was nervous as hell. He'd played out in his mind a hundred scenarios of how shit could go wrong. Jackson had given him a crash course in the business, so he felt confident about his abilities, but he wasn't sure about who, if anyone, to trust, especially when it came to his brothers and Emil. Hayden had already tried to play him, Jackson hated and resented him, and, Emil seemed too good to be true. In Antonio's mind, Emil had still let him into the fold too fast and too easily. Antonio knew he had to keep his guards up.

Just thinking about it, Antonio shifted in his seat and peered out of the long back window. The other vehicles were following close behind. He exhaled. For now, he could at least take comfort in the fact that all of their goons were in the vehicle directly behind him. Antonio knew his becoming a boss had left a lot of people unhappy. During the last meeting at the Blu with the crew and the customers who purchased their supply from Emil, Antonio said he would no longer be holding those type of long table meetings. After Gladstone's threat, Antonio thought it was too risky. His father-in-law could easily have him followed or bugged, and that would bring the entire operation down. Antonio was surprised that a man as smart and savvy as Emil had allowed those type of meetings anyway. "We are not the mafia. We are not some big time Mexican or Colombian cartel either. There is no need to risk ourselves by coming together like organized crime bosses. If you need something from us or we from you, we can arrange to meet privately in a setting that won't raise any red flags, but it won't be once a week," Antonio had announced during the last meeting.

Of course, his announcement was met with groans of protest, but he didn't let that faze him. The biggest protest came from Jackson, as expected. It would be the first of many decisions Antonio made without Jackson's input. There was always a fight after. Antonio was getting used to it. He had become adept at using Emil against Jackson, who was his brother's one weakness.

Antonio knew from listening to Jackson's story that all it took was one snitch to blow the lid on those meetings and law enforcement would be able to swoop in and pick up everyone at one time on RICO. He also knew Gladstone Tillary was always out to get the Cartwrights. Antonio promised himself he was going to finally find out why. For Antonio, risking all of your distributors at once was a stupid business move. A few men in the room that day hadn't been thrilled, especially because he'd also told them that the prices of the supply were going up twenty percent across the board on the instruction of Emil and Mo. Even though he was making more enemies than friends, he needed to find a quick way to recover the cost of the damage that had been done by Max King.

The convoy of vehicles had finally stopped. Antonio clenched his fists to calm the shaking in his hands. The vehicles had all stopped for a few seconds at a steel gate located at the end of a long alleyway. Aside from the scurrying rats and the glint of the city lights in the distance, the area was completely desolate. All of the surrounding industrial and factory-like businesses were shut down for the night and not set to open before the sun was shining bright in the sky. Antonio decided right away this was a place he would've never gone alone.

The two chain-linked gates in front of the vehicle moved open slowly like someone was operating them with a remote control. Each vehicle slowly inched forward. Antonio could hear rocks and gravel crunching under the SUVs wheels. A red brick, windowless warehouse sat on the dark waters of the New York Harbor. Some of Emil's men got out of the vehicle behind, guns in hand. Antonio went to grab the door handle closest to him. Jackson grabbed his arm, halting his movement. Antonio looked at him questioningly.

"Hold up. Let them do the sweep first," Jackson said seriously. Antonio's shoulders slumped. He felt like a stupid amateur. A few minutes later, one of Emil's workers tapped on the window and gave Jackson a hand signal.

"A'ight. We're clear. Bosses wait for doors to be opened for them," Jackson said with a smirk. He noticed how embarrassed Antonio was, and didn't miss the opportunity to exploit it.

"Whatever," Antonio grumbled.

The driver quickly jumped out and yanked the door open.

Antonio slid out of the car, Jackson at his side. They glided over to the center of the warehouse, their goons watching closely for any false moves.

Four young dudes approached from another vehicle. No surprise there. It seemed Mo's whole crew was comprised of young dudes. One kid stepped forward, his dark eyes trained on Antonio's face.

"You must be Antonio," the short kid said, his New York accent thick. Antonio nodded. "Cam . . . what up?" the kid introduced himself, extending his fists toward Antonio for a bump. Antonio did the same, bumping his fist with Cam.

"Mo asked me to let you know, he hopes this is the start of something good. He said to tell you what up and he didn't know you used to ball," Cam relayed.

"Tell him I appreciate it. You ready?" Antonio said, his tone kind of flat. He wanted to get to the business at hand.

He wasn't there to make small talk. Jackson had already warned him that some of these cats try to make small talk to throw you off your game. He told Antonio he needed to be stern and hold his ground, no matter what. Antonio could see Jackson boiling over, wanting to say something so badly. Two of Emil's guys retrieved two black duffel bags from the spare tire well in the back of the vehicle they had come in. Antonio could see the strain on their faces as they lugged the bags filled with cash.

Cam walked over, flanked by two of his young dudes. They all watched as Jackson unzipped the bags to reveal crisp new stacks of cash bound with thick red rubber bands and separated into twenty-thousand-dollar stacks.

"The first bag is for what we received last night on the first shipment. The second is the first half of what is owed for the past debacle," Antonio said smoothly, like he had been doing this for years. In actuality, his heart fluttered under his rib cage like a moth trapped in a jar. So far, he'd said exactly what he and Jackson discussed he should say. Antonio was definitely getting the hang of things.

"A'ight," Cam replied, handing the bags off to his partners. The three young dudes easily lifted each stack of cash, flicking through them as if they were decks of cards. Even as fast as they flipped, Antonio knew they were still being meticulous about the count.

"Straight," one of the young guys announced.

When they were done counting the money and secured the bags in their vehicle, Cam stepped closer to Antonio. Jackson moved in too, afraid he would miss something. That annoyed Antonio.

"Antonio, son. Mo wanted me to tell you one more thing," Cam said, almost regretfully. His eyes darted around wildly.

A cold sweat immediately broke out over Antonio's body. This was the bullshit he didn't want. No funny business. He raised his eyebrows in nervous anticipation of what was to come. Anything was possible in this business.

"What's up?" Jackson interjected, stepping to Cam.

Antonio put his hand on Jackson's shoulder. "It's cool. Let's hear him out."

"Listen, nigga don't shoot the messenger. Mo wanted me to tell y'all. I could care fucking less," Cam said, annoyed by Jackson's aggressive move.

Antonio shifted his weight from one foot to the next, listening intently.

"It's cool. Get to it," he huffed impatiently. He squeezed Jackson's shoulder as if to say, "Just chill."

"Mo wanted me to tell you that there is a traitor in your midst," Cam relayed, his words dropping like an atomic bomb.

"What? What, nigga? The fuck you talking about?" Jackson exploded, placing his left hand on his waistband.

Cam's young dudes moved in like ready soldiers, following his lead with their hands on their weapons as well. Cam stepped to the side of Jackson as if he was completely irrelevant.

"Antonio," Cam addressed him directly again, agitation lacing his words as he bit down into his jaw. "Mo asked me to deliver this as proof to his claims. Mo don't accuse niggas of shit unless he can back it up." Cam reached inside his pocket and removed a manila envelope.

All of Emil's men reacted by shifting in the distance behind Antonio, the metal of their weapons clicking and cocking. Antonio took a few steps back, not sure what the next move would be. Cam's young dudes did the same, holding their guns high and ready. Cam tossed the envelope onto the small metal table and stared at Antonio expectantly.

Antonio's heart jammed at the bone in his chest. His hands shook as he inhaled deeply. He swallowed the fear forming into a ball in his throat. *What the fuck is this they have?* Antonio's mind raced.

"Proof," Cam said calmly, folding his hands in front of him like a praying priest. Antonio hesitantly reached for the package.

"This is bullshit! They tryna play games right now! You don't have to look at shit they got to offer," Jackson came to life again, blocking the table and Antonio's access to the mysterious contents. "We came here to pay for the shipment. Period. All this extra shit is not needed!" Jackson barked his words out, his tone laced with panic.

Cam chuckled.

"A hit dog gon' bark my nigga," Cam said to Jackson as he eyed Jackson evilly. The only thing that kept Cam and his young dudes from blowing Jackson's head off was instructions from Mo to let Antonio handle his own business when it came to his family and their workers.

Antonio had to agree with what Cam had said to his men. Jackson seemed guilty and nervous about what might be in the envelope. Antonio stepped around Jackson and lifted the envelope. *There is a traitor in your midst. There is a traitor in your midst. There is a traitor in your midst.* The words played out in Antonio's mind like a scratched CD as he tore at the sealed envelope. He felt an uneasy tightness in his chest as he dumped six small three-by-five photographs into his hand. His mouth immediately fell open as he scanned the first picture. Antonio squinted to make sure his eyes weren't deceiving him. His head moved from side to side involuntarily, slowly.

"The fuck?" he whispered breathlessly. Heat rose from his toes up to his face and a sheen of red came over his eyes as if someone had put red-tinted glasses on him. He bit down into the side of his cheek as he flipped from one incriminating photograph to the next. Antonio looked over at Jackson, then back at Cam. His nostrils flared as he tried to keep his breathing under control.

"Where'd you get these?" he asked Cam, speaking through his teeth.

"A snitch we got working inside Max King's cartel turned the information over to Mo. Our people ran that shit down, and this is what we found out. We saved your fucking life today with this information, Antonio," Cam said seriously "If you cannot believe what's right there in your face, we have more proof that this is true," Cam said, raising his hand to one of his young dudes.

One of Cam's men, who looked like a big grizzly bear, rushed back toward their vehicle and snatched the hatchback door open. Antonio watched in utter shock as they dragged a guy out of the vehicle. The captive was quivering, blindfolded and gagged.

"Yo, nigga! What the fuck is this?" Jackson growled, his voice unsteady. Antonio looked around and saw that all of Emil's men and Jackson's so-called dudes were all on edge. Antonio could hear their angry murmurs.

"Nah, nigga. I feel a set up. Let's go," Jackson barked. "I'm not feeling this shit right here." The others mumbled their agreement. Jackson was ready to get the fuck out of dodge.

"Everybody shut the fuck up! Wait!" Antonio commanded. He still clutched the pictures against his chest as if he could make what he'd seen disappear.

The tall, dark haired guy was dragged from Cam's vehicle. Antonio sucked in his breath at the dude's poor condition. It immediately reminded Antonio of how he'd left his best friend Rich. His hands were bound tightly in front of him and he was being pushed toward Antonio on weak, shaky, bruised legs. He only wore his boxers and a bloodied t-shirt. Antonio could smell the fetid mixture of the guy's blood, shit, and piss emanating from his body. Someone had worked him over pretty damn good. Antonio winced just thinking about how much pain he must've been in. One thing was for sure: the nigga was scared to death. His eyes looked like two huge marbles, and his body quaked with fear.

"Speak up, nigga!" Cam barked, shoving the guy forward. Antonio looked at the guy's battered face—half shut eyes, his clearly broken nose, and his protruding, split upper lip. The abused guy refused to speak.

Cam nodded at his young goons. One of them rushed over, grabbed the tattered victim by his neck, and hoisted him off his feet. He squeezed the guy's throat until he was gagging.

"Put him down," Cam demanded. "Now . . . you tell him, motherfucker! I told you already . . . your fucking kid and bitch won't make it to see another fucking day!"

"The dude . . . he told me . . . he told me," the battered guy coughed, barely able to formulate words on his lips. He could barely speak. Antonio had to strain his ears to hear him.

"Speak the fuck up!" Cam barked, kicking the guy in his ribs so hard that everyone in the room winced.

"The dude . . . your dude . . . wanted to kill you. He . . . he . . . made a deal with Max King. He told me about this meeting today. He . . . he . . . set you up to be killed and robbed here today. He would get paid once we took the money and the shipment," the guy mumbled through his busted lips, blood dripping from his mouth onto the floor.

Antonio's mind screamed as his words hit home. He hadn't even been boss for more than a month, and someone in his own camp had already turned on him.

"What the fuck is they talkin' about, yo? I want to know what's going on right fucking now!" Jackson demanded, getting in Antonio's face.

Antonio's mind raced one hundred miles a minute. Everyone was vying for his attention. Jackson was screaming for an explanation. Cam was trying to convince him that what he was offering him was the truth. The guys were behind him yelling that they were ready to leave, that these young motherfuckers could not be trusted. It was all too much.

"Believe what you see in those pictures, my nigga. Mo is never wrong, and he never lies," Cam told Antonio calmly.

Antonio's body was engulfed in heat now. Something ticked at his core, like the timer on a bomb.

"I wanna know what the fuck he talkin' about," Jackson shouted, pulling his gun from his waistband. "I'm not fucking around no more."

Antonio felt like the room was spinning. He felt sick to his stomach. His ears rang.

"Shut the fuck up!" Antonio finally exploded, tossing the pictures back onto the table. "Everybody just shut the fuck up for a minute!" He slammed his hand on top of the pictures, spreading them out like a display of artwork.

"Satisfied?" Antonio huffed, placing the photographs in front of Jackson. He quickly fell silent. Antonio's eyes went into slits. He hated nothing more than liars, thieves, and traitors. All his life had been being betrayed.

"What? Nah," Jackson said, stepping back and shaking his head in disbelief. He took another close look at the pictures. "Nah, this fuckin' can't be!" Jackson growled, his words getting slightly louder. "Something gotta be fucking off here," he griped. His body went cold like someone had pumped ice water into his veins.

"The truth is all there," Cam instigated. "All I'm saying it's that nigga Mo expects you, as boss, to handle this," he said, looking directly at Antonio as he spoke.

Antonio knew that Cam would be reporting back to Mo exactly how he handled the situation.

Fuck! Fuck! Fuck!

His reputation depended on every single move he made now. Either he'd become known as a weak ass man in the business or a powerful force who could hold his own. It was up to him now. Antonio felt vomit creeping up his esophagus. Fire burned in his chest and huge sweat beads raced down his back. With his lips pursed and nostrils flaring, Antonio slipped his hand into his waistband. He wrapped his hand around the cold steel of the .357 Magnum Emil had given him. The one that Antonio never left home without these days. With his adrenaline rushing so fast, he turned toward the vehicles and stalked toward Emil's crew of men.

"What's going on, man?" one of them asked, his brows crumpled.

"Wait . . . what the fuck, Tony?" Jackson said, attempting to halt Antonio's fury. He was too late.

Antonio walked right up to the crew. None of them saw what was coming next. He raised his weapon and placed it at one of their men's temple. Everyone was speaking at once. There was an angry hornet's nest of buzzing in Antonio's ears. He felt like screaming as loud as his voice could go. The gun shook in his hand as it kissed the skin of the traitor's forehead.

Chaos erupted.

"What the fuck you doin'?" the man who always held Jackson down barked at Antonio with a two-gun salute.

Hayden's driver trained his gun on the traitor too. He was there as Antonio's muscle for the day. He took his lead from whomever was running the show as always. One of the other's pointed gun was leveled at Antonio's chest. After all, the identified traitor was around way before Antonio was. They'd all been working together before the outsider, Antonio, came on the scene. He was their brother in arms, and Antonio was just the new motherfucker who thought he was their boss. Another pointed his long gun, a shiny new AR-15, at Jackson. He couldn't understand how the fuck Jackson would choose Antonio over one of them . . . they'd been working for his father for decades.

"What the fuck?" the traitor growled, his hands up in surrender, weapon dangling off of his pointer finger. Clearly, he had no wins.

"Drop your weapon," Antonio said in a low, embittered whisper.

Jackson rushed over with the pictures in his hands. He didn't give a fuck about a gun pointed at him.

"Drop your fucking weapon now!" Antonio screamed this time, his voice getting so loud it itched the back of his throat. He thought about Mo for a hot minute. The secret Mo had harbored. He couldn't help but wonder how much else Mo knew that could be a danger to their family.

"Do what he said, man," someone yelled to the traitor. He was outgunned. He knew if he made one false move that would be his end.

"Explain yourself, motherfucker!" Jackson said angrily, making the pictures rain down around him. Everyone glanced down at the photographs. A bunch of mumbles and groans followed.

"What the fuck? This nigga is really a fucking traitor," one of them shouted. His words seemed to catch in the back of his throat.

"Is that you, nigga? You with dudes from Max King's crew—motherfuckers who tried to put us out of business?" Jackson asked, his voice cracking like he was about to cry.

Now, everyone turned their guns on the traitor. Their minds immediately went to thoughts of how close Max King had come to killing Emil one time. And how many times Max King had shut down Emil's operations. Was it the assistance of this fucking traitor that had caused Jackson to get arrested?

"Listen, I . . . I can explain," the traitor stammered. In their line of business, there really wasn't much more he could say that could help his case. The pictures did not lie.

"Y'all all agreed with me, remember? None of us wanted this intruder to be our boss. Don't front now!

C'mon, y'all remember what y'all said about how he didn't have no rights to come out of the blue and start taking over? How we all thought that shit wasn't right because we had all put in that work? Son or no son, this nigga didn't deserve to move up so fast! You said that! Jackson, remember you saying that he took over too fast and never acted like a son to your father? Didn't you think it strange that he was able to just meet Mo with no questions asked? Jackson, you hinted that you ain't trust him. I'm not fucking crazy! What the fuck, man? Y'all not gonna admit to shit now? I wasn't the only one that wanted to get rid of him. I did this for all of us! Max King said he was going to take care of him. This was for the fam!" the traitor cried out, snitching on his crew while his voice rose like a straight bitch.

Jackson looked at the man who had been in the car with him the day that he had seen Max King with Antonio's father-in-law, with the Senator. They were both stunned that there had been multiple people plotting on Antonio, but of course, they couldn't say anything now that someone else had taken the fall.

Antonio did believe that he had been the subject of many discussions. It wasn't lost on him that one of them—if not all of them—wanted to be the next boss in Emil's lineage. He couldn't let his feelings distract him, though. The issue at hand wasn't about who said what. Antonio needed to show them and Mo's youngins that he was first in command. His reputation as boss rode on how he handled this very moment.

"Nobody wanted me in this family? That's too bad, because I am a blood member. I'm here now, and you will all respect my authority. Like it or not," Antonio growled, flames flashing in his eyes. He ground the end of his gun on the traitor's temple.

"Please, don't kill me," the traitor begged. "That man they got tied up is Max King's nephew. If they kill him, you all will be dead men walking." The traitor knew he only had minutes to live. The warning was the least he could do to make up for his cowardly betrayal.

"Shut the fuck up! Don't give me no fucking advice now you fucking Judas!" Antonio growled, grinding his gun into the traitor's head even harder.

The man closed his eyes, waiting.

One of the other crew members turned away so no one could see the tears rimming his eyes. He was devastated by this betrayal, but even more about what he knew would happen next. Another man lowered his head as well.

"Let this be an example to the next man who tries us," Antonio shouted, putting pressure on the trigger.

One powerful blast to the dome spun the traitor's body around in a slow pirouette as a spray of his blood and gray brain matter splashed onto Antonio's face and clothes. The thick, metallic scent of blood mixed with the grit of gunpowder overwhelmed Antonio's senses. It was a smell and taste that surprisingly left him feeling powerful, almost animalistic. His jaw rocked feverishly.

Under the adrenaline rush, Antonio realized once again that he was someone who had tried to be good his entire life but was just as capable of killing a man in cold blood as any heinous murderer, under the right circumstances. Just like his father and his brothers. That fact scared the shit out of him.

Antonio gripped the gun and doubled over. Vomit spewed from his lips, just missing his shoes. His chest heaved like a beast in the wild after a fresh kill. Something inside of him had snapped. Antonio knew all too well how violence could be just as deep and intimate as love. In that moment, something awakened inside of him that he had worked years to suppress. He was turning into someone he didn't want to be, again. He hadn't realized with that one move, he had secured his family's fate.

Chapter 10

The Climax

Paige tucked Christian in to his makeshift bed and stood over him for a few minutes. Tears sprang to her eyes as she looked around. How far had things gone? How did her life go from charmed to fucked in a matter of months? Paige thought about the divorce, the press behind it, her family struggles, and it all made her cringe. Her father was currently going after Antonio and Emil Cartwright without mercy. Paige felt caught in the middle of it all. And, she definitely was.

"Hey," her brother, Junior, whispered, approaching from behind.

"Hey," Paige rasped, quickly wiping the tears from her face and putting on a fake smile. "I know you're put out, but thanks again for letting us crash with you so long. I'm trying my best to get things in order and as soon as I can. . . ."

"Shh. Stop worrying about me. I'm good," Junior cut in. "Look. We haven't always seen eye to eye. But, I know all of your tough love was because you didn't want me to be getting high and shit," he said, patting her shoulder. "Mi casa es su casa," Junior joked.

"I hope you do know that all of those times I was mean was out of love," Paige replied. She had been hard on her brother in the past when he'd go in and out of expensive drug rehabs. She always felt heartbroken over his addiction. He had embarrassed their family so many times that Gladstone had paid millions to public relations firms to get their family name back in a good light. Paige wondered why her father hadn't done anything about her name being dragged through the media as the wife of NBA-star-turned-criminal-boss.

"So, has the bastard even tried to contact you?"

"Oh, he's been trying. But after everything . . . he's lucky he's not in jail. The fucking nerve of him," Paige replied. Her mind was quickly drawn back to the night of the gala, the night her marriage went south for good.

"Don't bother coming home . . . we no longer have a home or a marriage!" Paige had hissed as she slung her body into her car.

Antonio had pounded on the window, but to no avail. Paige's tires squealed and she zoomed off so fast he had had to jump back or she would've run over his toes.

Antonio raced for his car and sped after her. She'd reached the house before he could, and when he'd gotten there she was in their walk-in closet, packing.

"Paige . . . let me talk to you," Antonio implored. "You know this is all bullshit. Just give me a minute to explain."

Paige kept moving swiftly. Her heart jammed so hard against her chest bone she felt like she'd faint.

"It's all not true," Antonio had said. "I didn't fuck her. I comforted her. She was sitting in her car before the fund-raiser, freaking about all that mess that had happened with Rod. So, I went and talked to her. I was just trying to be a good friend. But that was it. What makes you think I'd do some shit like that? With your best friend?" He knew that he was lying, he knew that she knew he was lying, but he couldn't stop himself. Paige was the last thing that he had, and he knew that if she knew for sure, that if he confirmed what she thought was true, it was over. He thought about an alternative defense, that maybe if he explained that she had come on to him, Paige would be lenient, but he knew that it wouldn't matter.

Paige had finally stopped moving and stared straight across the car at her husband. The knot that had formed in her chest finally unraveled like a ball of yarn that had been dropped. He must think that she was stupid.

"You know what Antonio? You're a fucking liar."

"I'm not!" he had said spiritedly. He was falling deeper and deeper into his lie. He put his hands up. "Why is this different? You always at least listen to me. You always at least try to understand my side." He could feel how ridiculous he sounded, but he couldn't stop. Paige's face went dark, and for the first time ever, he could see that she was her father's daughter.

"You stupid piece of shit. you stupid fucking piece of shit. What is this then?" Paige flew over to Antonio, and for a second he thought that she was going to hit him, but instead she launched her manicured hands into his shirt and pulled on his collar so hard it ripped at the seams. Antonio fell back.

"What are you talking about?" he yelled, trying to pull his shirt back to the way that it should be.

"Look in the fucking mirror," Paige said, her voice heavy with malice. Antonio walked backward and positioned himself so that he could see the part of his neck that Paige had exposed. Right under his shirt collar, barely noticeable, was a hickey. He could have kicked himself right then and there. All that time spent defending his lie, trying to protect Paige's feelings, and he had just made himself look worse and worse with each word. He looked at Paige, and the light had gone out in her eyes. They both knew that his performance earlier had only dug him deeper into the hole.

"You are a sociopath and I will no longer go along with your lies. I will not continue in this marriage with you. You will not embarrass me anymore. It's bad enough that you keep getting traded from teams, then you get cut, and then woman after woman. Let's not even mention you getting caught drinking and driving, and all of staying out late at night you've been doing when you *should* be looking for a damn job . . . a real damn job. Be a real man like my father for once in your fucking life," Paige had unleashed, jutting her finger accusingly at Antonio. She regretted the words immediately after they spilled from her mouth. Like always. But there would be no turning back.

Over the years, she had kept a lot of her real feelings to herself so that Antonio wouldn't feel emasculated by her or her family. Or, made to feel like he was living in the shadows of her father. But the dam of restraint she had built had finally broken that night, leaving nothing but the ugly truth spewing from her mouth. Paige had had enough.

"Embarrass you any more than I already have?" Antonio had repeated, his words slightly slurred. "That's what you're going with Paige? I embarrass you? Be like your father? The man who cheats on his wife openly, plays on both sides of the legal system, and would step on all of your necks to get ahead? That's who I should aspire to be?" Anger flared and flashed in Antonio's eyes. Paige recognized that look, but she didn't care. He had started this fight, but she would finish it. He'd committed the worst crime against their marriage he possibly could, so fuck it . . . the gloves had come all the way off.

"Fuck you, Antonio! Team after team. City after city. I followed you like a good wife, but you ruined everything. You let your past break our future. You wanted to run around with your hood friend who burned the shit out of you. He took everything, because you were too stupid not to be loyal to someone like him. But me . . . you couldn't ever be loyal to me! Now you want to run behind a father who never wanted you. Again . . . loyal to people who don't give a fuck about you! And Michaela? You think she cares anything about you or me? She's selfish! You knew this for years! You're a fucking total failure, Antonio! You failed at making your mother proud and you certainly fucking failed me as a wife!" Paige spat, all the veins in her face visible. Tears covered her face and spit had flown out of her lips. She was shaking like mad.

Antonio's fingers curled into fists.

"Don't ever mention my mother," Antonio snarled. "You're not worthy to even say her name. She was a real woman who held it down without a man . . . something you don't know shit about. You went from depending on your daddy to depending on me! What the fuck can you say you contributed to this marriage? It was *my* career that provided for you all this time. And now you got the nerve to act like I don't matter? You just gonna say shit out of your mouth. I didn't sleep with her! You ever think that our marriage failed because you were too busy buying material shit and not taking care of my needs? You think I wanted to chase pussy? You think I wanted to find happiness in the bottom of a fucking bottle, Paige?"

Paige chortled. "Oh, now it's my fault. I stick in this shitty game we call a marriage for the optics of it all, but frankly, I'm fucking embarrassed by you. You ain't no fucking real man, no, you're a sorry excuse for one," Paige said maliciously. The words had rolled off her tongue so fluidly she had to wonder who she'd become.

Antonio jerked his head back as if Paige's words were a stinging bite from a poisonous cobra. He was on the move before she could even blink twice. Paige hadn't been able to move out of his path as he barreled toward her like a bull on the charge. She let out a short-lived scream as Antonio grabbed her neck and squeezed it.

Paige had smelled the liquor hot on Antonio's breath. She had seen the rage and fire flashing in his eyes. Fear had come over her until she felt like she was going to die.

"Bitch! I took care of you even when I was feeling like shit about myself! I did the best I could, but nothing, *nothing* was ever fucking good enough for you!" Antonio boomed, breathing in her face with tears rimming his eyes. He was cutting off Paige's air supply.

Paige swung her arms wildly and caught him across the right cheek with her fingernails. "Let me go, Antonio!" Paige had croaked out. Her throat had felt scorched.

"You have no fucking respect for me. All I ever did was try," Antonio grunted, still gripping her neck.

Paige dug her nails into his hands and spit at him. "Please," she whispered. "You're going to kill me."

It was as if Antonio had gone to another place and then suddenly returned. He quickly released his grip on Paige's neck and put his left hand up to his cheek and felt blood dripping from the welts on his face. Paige dropped to the floor, gasping and wheezing. Antonio shook his head.

"This is what we've come to? How? How Paige?" Antonio had croaked out, his mouth dry like he had hands full of sand. Paige had sobbed so hard it took her a few seconds to gather herself.

"You made us come to this," she had said through tears.

"Right. It's always my fault. Always," Antonio said, his voice low and mournful.

He put his hands over his face and sobbed for what they'd become. For what he'd become. He hadn't cried in years—not since he'd lost his mother. It was one thing for Antonio to know the violence of killing a man, of taking a life, but putting his hands on a woman, let alone the mother of his child, was something that he never thought he could have done. But he had, and he hadn't even realized it.

Tears had leaked from Paige's eyes, and she couldn't move. She could barely catch her breath and her entire body had felt tense. Antonio was very lucky. For now. Her father was a powerful man. He wouldn't take kindly to Antonio putting his hands on her like that. Antonio had never done anything like that before, and Paige wanted him to know that it was not going to ever happen again.

"It's over. I want a divorce and I never want to see you again," Paige rasped, barely able to get the words out from her bruised neck. "I will never be your wife again after today."

"Sis, you don't look too good," Junior said, breaking up Paige's nightmare.

She shook her head. "No, no, I'm fine." She smiled weakly.

"I'd say that's a stretch, but, if you say so," her brother shrugged. "I have to run out for a few. Just try to get some rest." He gave her a short side squeeze.

Paige looked up with tears in her eyes. "Thank you, Junior. I love you."

"Don't hurt my mommy! Get off of her!" a little voice screeched, pure terror underlying every word.

Paige thought she was dreaming. She could hear her son Christian's voice as her eyes fluttered open.

"Yo, you just gonna stand there lookin' dumb? Shut that fuckin' kid up. Matter of fact, take him out of here while I handle this right here! I can't even fuckin' think straight with all that hollering," a man's voice growled.

Paige's eyes flew open, only to find herself staring down the barrel of a gun and two men standing over her. The other man immediately went into action, holding Christian around the waist like he was a little rag doll.

"Mommy! I want my mommy!" Christian screamed as he kicked, squirmed, and stretched his arms in the direction of Paige.

At the sound of her son's distress, Paige went into attack mode, like a mother bear in the wild protecting her young from a predator. She clawed, kicked, and writhed fiercely against one of the men's grip. Her petite frame was no match for the bodybuilder biceps of her attacker.

Paige moaned against the leather-gloved gorilla hand that covered her nose and mouth. She tried to drop her weight in an attempt to ease out of his grasp, but that also proved futile.

"Keep still bitch! If you wanna save yourself and save your kid, you better keep the fuck still!" the man spat, his shitty breath hot and stale against Paige's ear. The mention of her son and the terrifying thought that something might happen to him, made Paige go still for a few minutes. The man's accomplice carried her son, kicking and screaming toward another room in the house.

"I want my mommy! Stop! Mommyyyyy!" Christian screamed until he lost his breath.

Paige moaned loudly. She couldn't stop the tears from flowing down her face now. With a gun pressed to her spine, there was not much she could do for her son right now. Her body quaked with emotion. Her legs weakened, but her will to live and to protect her son from these goons grew by the minute.

"Yo! Don't hurt a hair on his fucking head. The boss wants him as leverage. We ain't tryna fuck this up," the leader of the two assailants yelled out to his partner as he kept Paige in a tight grip.

Paige was crying so hard she could barely catch her breath. Every time she sucked in, she'd get a mouth and nose full of the odor of the filthy, worn leather of the man's glove.

"Yeah, now back to you. So, I heard you're a little kept rich princess. I heard your daddy is supposed to be the shit and your man thinks he's the shit," the masked assailant hissed as he held her from behind and spoke directly into her ear.

Paige felt his dick growing against her ass as he spoke. Her stomach immediately curdled. She wanted to vomit.

"I think before it's all said and done, I wanna know what it's like to fuck a rich bitch. Maybe I'll let your little bitch ass boy live, if I can get some of that tight, rich, stuck up pussy. Whatchu think? I heard you rich bitches got the prettiest pussies around. Is your shit pretty?" he provoked. His own lecherous thoughts distracted him enough that he removed his gun from Paige's back and shoved it into the back of his pants. He needed a free hand so he could fondle her perfect, ample breasts. He was already going against the specific instructions he'd been given—get in, do the deed, get the kid and the bitch, and leave. He thought he might as well enjoy himself a bit before getting the job done.

Paige cried out as the man's hands slithered like a venomous snake over her body. He pinched her nipples and ran his tongue over her neck and ear. She felt so sick to her stomach a little bit of vomit crept up her throat. She closed her eyes and thought about Christian.

"Dayum . . . you taste so good. Hard to believe your stupid ass husband left you. I guess that it don't matter now. I'll be your husband for a few minutes," he hissed, invading her crotch with rough hands.

Paige pleaded for him to stop but he had tuned all of her noises out. She could still hear her son crying out for her from some place in the house. When he was a baby, Paige never let him cry. She would hold him close until he was calm enough to be put back down. People claimed she spoiled the boy too much, but she never wanted him to feel abandoned or alone. Now, unable to comfort him, his little cries cut through her like a million knives. Paige said a quick silent prayer that if God let her survive this attack she would find out who was responsible and reign sheer terror on their life.

"A'ight, miss rich bitch. We can try this the easy way, or the hard way." The man briefly removed one of his hands from Paige's body to reach into his back pocket. Paige saw a small window of opportunity and decided she would jump on it. With a boost of courage that could've only been sent from God, Paige lifted her foot and brought her heel down on top of the man's foot with all of the force she had in her slim body.

Shocked by her actions, the perverted intruder startled. Paige took her elbow and reared it back into the man's rib cage with so much force she felt something in her own arm pop. That backed the man up. She used her bony elbow for one more driving stab to his midsection.

"You bitch!" the man screamed in pain. Paige was able to get out of his grasp as he stumbled backward a few steps. She completely knocked the wind out of him. Thinking of her son propelled her forward.

"Help! Help me!" Paige screamed at the top of her lungs, running straight for her brother's front door. She figured if she could get one of the neighbors to hear her cries they'd at least call the police. Right now, she needed to work on getting her son away from the other attacker. Paige ran to the front door but quickly realized that deadbolt was in place. Junior had always told her to put it on the door to keep her and Christian safe and now it was the one thing standing in the way of her freedom, she was trapped inside.

"Please!" she cried, still facing the door as if her cries could magically open the lock.

"Oh, you fucked up now!" the masked man barked as he took ogre-like steps toward her. "You looking for this key? You dumb bitch!" He was on her within seconds. Paige felt his weight crash into her from behind. She hit the floor with so much force she saw small flashing stars squirming in the corners of her eyes. Her will to live and her desire to save her son were stronger than any common reasoning. Paige planned to fight to the bitter end, if necessary.

Somebody help me!" Paige kicked and clawed at the beast on top of her. She swiped at the man's face mask, but she couldn't pull it all the way off. She managed to claw a chunk of skin from his exposed neck, however.

The man roared like an angry bear. "You 'bout to get yourself fucked up!" he growled like a hungry wolf, slamming his fists into the delicate bones of her face. Paige felt her skin split like the seam of a fat man's pants. An explosion of pain vibrated through her entire skull. The hit rendered her temporarily immobile.

"Help me," she gasped, not able to get enough air in her lungs this time to even speak. Paige had put up a good fight. Her face was now a bloodied mess and her head pounded. She could feel her eye slowly closing. It was all for nothing. The other man came rushing back into the room, his gun out in front of him.

"Yo! What the fuck, man? This is taking too fucking long!" he said, beginning to panic. "I'm sick of sitting in there with that crying ass kid! I don't care whose kid it is, if that fucka don't stop screaming I'ma silence him for real!"

"Shut the fuck up and help me. This bitch just tried to escape!"

"Keep on fighting us and your baby is a goner," the man who held Paige's son captive warned as he assisted his accomplice with subduing her. Paige stopped dead after she heard those words. If it meant saving her son's life, she would do whatever they asked her to do.

The leader of the two, the one she'd fought aggressively, hoisted her up from the floor by her hair.

"I see you wanna play hard to get. Don't you know that payback is a bitch?" The man wheezed between breaths. "Help me tie this bitch up!"

Within minutes, Paige was in a helpless position with extension cords binding her to a kitchen chair. A wet dishcloth was shoved into her mouth and tied in place with string that usually held her recycled newspapers together. Paige hung her head. What had she done to deserve this? Paige couldn't think of any legitimate reason for the attack today.

"Now, like I was saying before you fucked up and thought you could make it out of here in one piece . . ." the leader said, yanking her head up by her hair. He clearly took great pleasure in her suffering. A sick bastard. That's who stood before her. Paige looked into his eyes with her one good eye. His eyes seemed eerily familiar. It was the only part of his face she could see, really.

"I heard your family got money. Is that true or not?" he growled, yanking her head in a full circle so hard she heard something at the base of her skull crack.

"Mmmm hmmmm . . ." Paige moaned, shivering. All she wanted to know was if her son was okay. She pictured his innocent doe eyes, perfect button nose, and heart shaped lips and began to struggle all over again.

"Good, 'cause we gon' try out that pussy right now," he spat, his words like a reptile's tongue hissing against her ear.

Suddenly she heard the locks on the door clicking. Paige's heart almost stopped. *Junior!* She began bucking against the restraints, but it was too late. Her brother walked right into a trap. The two men descended on Junior like lions on an unsuspecting antelope.

"No! Junior!" Paige muffled behind the restraint. It was too late. One of the attackers slammed his gun into Junior's head and knocked him out.

"Oh, this must be the druggie brother they told us about," one of the attackers snarled. "They said he might be here. And we got just the thing for his ass."

Paige's eyes grew wide. She watched in terror as the attacker pulled the small orange stopper off of a slim syringe. Tears burst from the sides of her eyes and urine leaked over her tied legs and feet. Fear was choking off her air supply. That small needle was worse in her eyes than any other torture method the man could have used against her brother.

Paige groaned loudly, trying her best to scream out through the gag. She struggled against the restraints, muscles and veins tight against her skin. She moved so fiercely the chair scraped against the tiled floor. She shook her head frantically from side to side. Her eyes were stretched to their limits. Paige started gagging on the rag stuffed in her mouth.

"What you scared of? This that shit he loves right here? I heard he was clean . . . oh well, you know what they say— one hit gets them back to square one," the man laughed evilly, moving toward Junior with the syringe like a death penalty executioner holding the lethal injection.

Paige begged through the cloth in one last-ditch effort for even an ounce of compassion. Paige knew that for Junior, what the man was holding might as well have been something that would stop his heart . . . he might as well have put a gun to Junior's head and blown his brains out.

Paige knew each time around, her brother moved closer and closer to never kicking the habit again. Once he got that first taste, it might all be over for him. The man walked over, grabbed her head, and forced her to watch. Paige moaned and tried to move.

"You need to fucking watch or everybody dies. If you fuck around and move, he's a goner," he said as he held her head until she couldn't look away. Paige stopped fighting. For her, it was already over. This man was obviously the devil and hell bent on destroying her entire family. But, why?

"This seems like a good one," he said, placing the syringe against Junior's skin. Paige wanted to close her eyes at the pinprick of the syringe in her brother's body. The man pushed the plunger on the back of the syringe slowly. His eyes glistened with deviant pleasure. He held onto her head as she watched her brother's body react.

The drugs shot straight to his nervous system. His entire body tensed at first. Junior's eyes groggily blinked open and rolled up into his head until only the whites were visible. Then his body went slack. The attacker released Paige's hair, letting her head drop until her chin was touching her chest. She sobbed as she watched her brother fall into a dope fiend slump, a sight Paige had fought every day to forget.

"Yeah, that's the shit right there, ain't it? I thought this nigga might OD on this pure-ass shit, since I heard he ain't had it over a year. But seems like he still got that strong, resilient system. They say this girl is the devil and all it takes is one taste and a nigga will forget he was clean for any amount of time," the man said slyly, proud of his work.

"Now, back to you. You owe me something," he said smoothly. He took the dishrag out of Paige's mouth. Her lips trembled. He took that as his opportunity to have his way. Paige could hear his zipper coming down. She could even smell his musty balls. But, she had no strength to fight. She had given up. Paige didn't forget that she had a little boy and that he needed her, but she felt completely helpless. The man shoved his dick into her mouth with a forcefulness that had her gagging. Paige couldn't even feel any way about it. She thought about biting his dick off, but before the thought could materialize, the man pulled out three more little syringes, full to the brim.

"These are for him. You try anything slick, he gets all three, and then you'll never see your son again," the man said cruelly.

"No, please," she whispered. Her head rocked from side to side. Tears ran in steady streams out of her eyes. The man untied her, and she didn't even try to fight again. She curled up in a ball in the floor like a fetus in her mother's womb.

Chapter 11

All Falls Down

Hayden's naked body shivered. His ass throbbed from sitting on whatever icy, cold surface his captors had him on. His wrists and ankles were bound together. He managed to pull his knees up to his chest to generate some kind of heat from his thighs. Somewhere in the distance, he could hear water dripping. A slow, steady drip. It was starting to make him go crazy. It seemed like forever since he'd been snatched as he walked into his expensive condo building.

Hayden could hear voices speaking in muffled whispers. He lifted his head from his knees, wincing because his neck was stiff. Footsteps approached, and his heart began to race.

"Hello?" Hayden rasped. Something about the conditions of the room was getting to his head. He could swear he heard his father's voice too. That would be impossible.

"One of the infamous Cartwright boys, eh?" a lanky man said, standing in front of Hayden.

"Whatever you want, my father will give it up to get me free," Hayden rambled through bluish-purple lips. He could barely speak through his chattering teeth.

"What I want is in your head. No one can pay for that." Hayden knew right away what that meant—the man wanted him to give up the inside goods about his father and their business. Hayden and Jackson had spent their entire lives being warned about this type of scenario. Hayden never heeded the warnings since he was head of all of the legitimate businesses. He was stupid. It made sense that they'd snatch him . . . the most likely to have his guard down.

"So, tell me—the boss—you like him?" the man asked. Hayden didn't answer; instead, he hung his head. They were looking for information about Antonio.

"You won't speak? Do you know who sent me?" the man asked. Hayden kept his head bowed. "Get him up!"

Three men moved in on Hayden like zookeepers attempting to tame a wild animal. Hayden grunted as they forced his stiff, frozen body off the floor. His skin was sensitive to the touch, almost frostbitten. With a man flanking him on each side, Hayden was held upright. The freezing cold air in the room stung his entire body. His legs dropped from the bent position, leaving his chest and genitals exposed to the frigid conditions.

"Now, I know you feel very cold. Let's change that," the man said. He pulled out a double spouted blowtorch and turned the feeder knob. A blast of fire burst from the end. Hayden's eyes flew open, frozen puffs of breath escaping his lips.

"Aggghhh!" he screeched at the top of his lungs as the flame drew closer. The man let out a maniacal laugh as he turned the torch off.

"So, back to my questions. Your new boss, I think he's your brother, do you like him? I want to know some things about him," the man asked again. Hayden did not respond. He closed his eyes and started praying silently.

The man cursed. Hayden could hear the torch being sparked up again. His body tensed. The men lifted him up a little higher so that his chest was almost eye level with the torch.

"You could save yourself—this is your last chance," the man hissed. Hayden didn't respond. He'd partially betrayed Antonio once, and he'd regretted every day since then. He wasn't going to do it again. Especially because he felt like they'd kill him anyway.

The man squinted his eyes and moved closer. He sprayed the torch flame up and down the frozen skin on Hayden's chest. The sound Hayden released from his mouth was not of this Earth. His body bucked wildly. The man moved the flame from Hayden's chest, and large blisters immediately popped up on his seared skin.

"Max King. Have you heard of him?" the man continued with his questions.

Hayden's head hung, and saliva dripped out of his mouth. His body vibrated with unleashed pain. Was it possible to feel both hot and cold at the same time?

"Answer me or I'll be forced to turn this thing back on," the man warned. "I know you know who my boss is, correct?"

Hayden moved his head in the affirmative. The effort caused his entire body to burn with pain.

"Good, good. King wants to know about your boss," the man continued.

Hayden shook his head from side to side, but didn't utter a word.

"Turn him!" the man shouted in disgust.

The men holding Hayden shifted him so that the skin on his back was exposed to the interrogator.

"You will tell me what I need to know." The torch spit fire onto Hayden's back, buttocks and thighs. Hayden heard his skin sizzling like meat in a frying pan.

"When you have frostbite it is always wise to stay away from heat for a while. If not, the skin dies and has to be cut off. First we freeze you; then we burn you," the man snarled.

"Okay! Okay! Please . . . stop." Hayden pleaded with his captors, no longer able to withstand the torture.

The man removed the torch from Hayden's skin, and the other two men turned Hayden around.

"You will tell me all I need to know, or you will die a very painful death. Do we understand each other, now?"

Hayden moved his head. His lips trembled as he uttered the one word that could end his current state of misery.

"Yes."

Five broad-shouldered men stood guard inside the Burge, a repair shop that was owned by the Cartwrights. Tonight, a hundred boxes of SUV and luxury car parts would be loaded with eighty-percent pure cocaine for shipment to various distributors. Jackson and Antonio had agreed to oversee the operation together. Mo had instructed Antonio to go it alone, but he'd made his brother a promise that he'd involve him in all aspects of the new business.

The heroin was strategically placed between the metal spokes and wheel beds of the rims and the engine wells. Jackson paced through the shop like a prison warden. A few times, he climbed into the backs of the trucks to personally ensure the packaging was on point. Antonio was impressed with Jackson's dedication. Antonio was learning.

Jackson looked at his Rolex for the third time. They were three minutes over the allotted sorting and packing time, and every second counted.

"Yo! Put a fuckin' move on it. We do this shit on a time limit. Slipping up is how shit gets murky! Nothing can be off, right now. This is going to be the biggest move we've made in years," Jackson announced to the paid help, who needed to step up their packing game.

One of the men walked over to Jackson, sweat dripping down the side of his face. He wiped his face with the sleeve of his shirt.

"This is crazy, man. This is a lot more than we ever shipped at one time. The time window ain't cuttin' it. We need at least twenty more minutes. Only truck one is finished, and we're only halfway through with truck two. This shit is mad over the top. You know, that's easily over two million dollars that's gonna be out there for the taking," the dude huffed, scowling. "What's the fuckin' rush?"

Antonio stepped forward to address the worker, but Jackson threw his hand up and moved up himself.

"Yo! You sound like a whining ass bitch right now. A hundred boxes or ten boxes, the shit still gotta be delivered to the streets, right? I ain't got all night to be in here watching grown ass men complain and shit," Jackson grumbled, looking at his watch again. Secretly, he was sweating under his clothes too. The dude was right. This operation was much larger in scale than what they'd attempted before.

"Man, look. This y'all operation. I do my part and I don't ask no questions, feel me? But this shit is risky right now. You better tell ya fuckin' new boss to take some classes in this street game next time and have his ass here to see to his own fuckin' business."

Venting complete, the dude stalked off to finish the job. Antonio smirked. He wouldn't even give the dude any lip service. Also, unfazed by the crybaby, Jackson looked at his watch one more time. He was on a time constraint of his own, but the way shit was going, he would have to scale back his own plans. Jackson walked into the shop's office and locked the door behind him. He pulled the string on the white metal vertical blinds that hung over the large front window of the shop.

Jackson pulled out his cell phone and dialed the number. No answer.

"Fuck!" he huffed and began pacing. His plans were being derailed, and the price would be very heavy. "One more try," he spoke under his breath to himself. Jackson hit the call button again. When the line picked up, he let out a long breath and relaxed the tension in his shoulders.

"Pop, I know what you said you wanted to happen, but this shit is going way over, the timing ain't gon' be right for this one. Maybe we can do it on the next one," Jackson hurriedly conveyed the message.

He patiently allowed for the tongue-lashing he received. Jackson closed his eyes and pinched the bridge of his nose with his free hand. If only he could just tell his father everything he wanted to tell him all of these years. First, he forced Antonio on them, and now, he wanted to make him prove himself worthy despite everything he had done for the business.

"This one just didn't pan out. Let's try one more time with something that's gonna be a sure bet. Plus, it ain't gonna shake him up. The nigga is here and clueless," Jackson said calmly, trying his best to hold his composure.

Jackson exhaled a windstorm of breath. He wasn't going to tolerate too many more "assholes" and "stupid fucks" from his father. The idea was dumb anyway, staging a raid to see how Antonio would handle it, seemed to Jackson to be somewhat childish. Setting up his own flesh and blood: that was the kind of man Emil Cartwright was.

"I'll let you know about the next go 'round," Jackson said before quickly hanging up.

A knock sounded at the door, causing him to startle.

"Yo!" Jackson hollered, bopping over to the door.

"You a part of this or what?" Antonio asked, stealthily scanning the office with his eyes.

"Are you questioning me, now?" Jackson snapped right back. The entire crew had been suspicious of one another since the last incident. Antonio was especially suspicious of everyone, even his brothers.

"This shit was a rush job, but everything is set to roll out. Two to the Hanover and one to Southeast, just like always," informed Jackson.

"Yeah, that's the flow as usual. You ride with the two. Sill will roll with the other. Once all the collections have been made, y'all can meet up and make the split at the Blu," Antonio instructed.

"And you?" Jackson asked, tapping his foot like a mother waiting for an answer from a disobedient child.

"Me what? I'm goin' the fuck home," Antonio snarled. "You said you wanted the biggest part in this shit, right? Well, you got it."

Jackson walked out of the office, Antonio following on his heels. They did a quick walk-through of the shop and made sure all three trucks were ready for departure.

Jackson approached the driver's side window of the first truck. He nodded at the driver and tossed a rubber-banded stack of cash at the man.

"Get this shit there, or else," he warned. It was the same shit his father had said each time he sent a man out for delivery. Emil had joked with his sons that it was a good luck send off. "Scare a motherfucker before you send him, and he'll bring you back what you need."

Jackson walked over and climbed into his car. The shop's metal gates began to roll up. Both trucks were idling as they waited for him.

Jackson reversed his car out of the driveway and waited for Antonio to do the same. As the first truck made its way out of the garage, tires squealed nearby. Jackson jerked as he heard the rapid-fire chattering of bullets ripping through the air. Jackson felt trapped as

the "tat-tat-tat" of gunfire hit the exterior shell and glass
windows of the shop.

Jackson threw his car in reverse and slammed on
the accelerator. His car sped backward, away from the
gunfire. He looked up just in time to see an army of men
in black rushing toward the shop. Antonio's car was still
inside.

Jackson hurriedly swiveled his car around and drove
away from the danger. His chest felt like it was going
to cave in. Jackson couldn't think straight. His hands
shook so badly he could hardly drive. After several failed
attempts, he managed to hit the Bluetooth function in his
car.

"Call Pop!" Jackson screamed at the machine.

"Yeah?" Emil answered, his voice laced with aggrava-
tion.

"Yo!" Jackson hollered, unable to even find the words.

"Jax?" Emil replied, his tone an octave higher than
before.

"Yo, somebody just hit up the shop. I think they got
Antonio, man," Jackson stumbled for the right words.

"What? What the fuck?" Emil cussed, on his feet within
seconds. "Who? Who was it? Is he dead? Did they grab
him? What about the shipments?"

"I don't fuckin' know! All I saw was a black truck
pull up and a flood of dudes in black with AKs and MPs
sparkin' off, straight for the trucks. Tony pulled his whip
up and was right there. We are under fuckin' attack, Pop!
Meet me at the Blu. This shit is bad. I really think it was
King!" Jackson spat angrily. The Cartwrights were under
attack. Shit was going downhill fast. The war had been
calm thus far, but this game was about to be over.

"I want somebody from Max King's crew dead *tonight*!"
Emil barked as he paced across the meeting room at the
Blu.

Jackson sat with his eyes closed and his hands steepled in front of him. Their crew members had burners on the table, barely able to control their impulse to kill.

"You sure you wanna make such a big decision? A war between us and King would leave us all open to the young fucks we just got down with. This Mo motherfucker supposed to be a big dog," one of the guys called out from the back of the room.

Emil sucked in his breath and shot him a cold stare. He was always sensitive when people questioned his executive decisions.

"It was King! We don't have beef with nobody else for no other reason. They left the fuckin' shipment for the Feds to find. If it was just a robbery, you think that would be the case?" Jackson boomed, his face hot with anger. A wave of groans rose and fell around the room.

Whoever had shot up the shop hadn't taken any of the drugs, just killed all three drivers and all five guards. Antonio had apparently gone missing, but his car was found inside with a spray of bullet holes on its side.

By now, the shop was surely crawling with police and narcs. Emil and Jackson would probably have to deal with the cops and Feds since all of their businesses were currently under scrutiny. They'd also have to deal with Mo now that the heat was literally crawling up their asses.

"I don't care how y'all do it. I don't care who you gotta speak to. I want somebody that is key to Max King hit tonight! I need to know by tomorrow that Antonio is safe. And, where the fuck is Hayden?" Emil announced and asked at the same time. "Go! Everybody get the fuck to work!"

The men filed out of the room, except for Jackson.

"You all right?" Emil asked Jackson. He looked like he had aged ten years overnight.

"I almost got my fuckin' head blown off and my brother is missing . . . probably dead somewhere. Nah, I'm not all right. Life as we know it ain't never gon' be the same. If you didn't know it before, you damn sure know it now. Pop, this is a fuckin' declaration of war."

"Change happens every day. I was forced into this business when I was a boy. Now I'm responsible for my own empire. If it's war they want, it's war they will get," Emil shot back. Even he wasn't sure how he was really going to handle Max King, but he wasn't about to let anyone know that he didn't have all of the answers. Not even his son.

"Yeah, exactly. But we need to be smarter than them this time," Jackson grumbled, pushing his chair back, putting a new dent in the wall. He stormed out.

The Cartwright empire was shrinking quickly. They needed to find more trusted knights to protect their castle before it was overrun by their many enemies.

Chapter 12

Ties That Bind

Antonio shivered as blood ran down his face, chest, and stomach. He couldn't stop his legs from shaking, and he felt like his bladder would explode at any moment. Wherever they had him, it was literally freezing cold, like he was naked in Alaska.

"Hit him again," a man's voice boomed. Antonio braced himself, because he knew exactly what was coming next. "Please," he whispered, but that was for nothing. It was clear that these very dangerous people were not going to have any mercy on him. It was also clear that if he ever got out of there, he would hunt down each and every one of them and kill them one by one, slowly and painfully.

Antonio let out another scream as he felt the shock waves from the oversized stun gun. His face folded into a pain-filled frown, and his eyes rolled into the back of his head. Sweat was pouring from every pore on his body. He gagged, but nothing came up from his stomach. His heart pounded painfully against his chest bone. Antonio was wishing for death, because even that had to be better than what he was feeling. Another hit with the electric current caused piss to spill from his bladder and splash on the feet of one of his captors.

"This bitch ass nigga pissed on me!" the thug growled. Then he took his huge fist and punched Antonio across the face so hard spit shot out of his mouth.

"Antonio! Help us!"

The words, the sound, the voice, almost made Antonio's heart burst. Fuck the pain he was feeling from another hit from the stun gun, nothing was worse than hearing Paige screaming for his help. Then he heard his son's cries. Antonio squinted and saw Christian and Paige huddled together, a gun at their heads.

"Please let her go," he mumbled, his words coming out labored and almost breathless. "Just take me, but let her go," he whispered through his battered lips. It was almost unreal what they were going through. As hard as the torture was, it was even harder for Antonio to see Paige and his son in a position of total helplessness. He had always been his son's hero. When Antonio's mother died, he'd promised himself that when he became a parent, he would be the best at it. He would make any and all sacrifices to take care of his son. Antonio thought he was always so strong and heroic to Christian, but now, he was just as weak and useless.

"Antonio," Paige panted. "Don't let them kill us."

Antonio squinted through his battered eyes and tried to see them again, but the bright lights his torturers were using prevented him from catching a good glimpse of his family. Whether they were divorced or not, Paige and Christian were really the only family Antonio had. He'd fucked up, and he knew that now. All he wanted was another chance to make it right. He figured that he would probably never see them again. He could hear their voices around him clearly though, so he knew they were all in close proximity.

"Unfortunately for you, your father betrayed me. It is inevitable that the sins of the father fall on the sons," a man Antonio couldn't see said in an eerily calm voice.

"Agh!"

Antonio startled to the sound of Hayden's screams. They had them all there.

"I tried everything in my power. But, that old Emil, he just kept on coming into territory that wasn't his. I should have never trusted him as a business partner. I should have known that such a weak man, who would run from his being a father to his own son, who would betray his own fucking blood, could never be a good partner. And then . . . I tried another route. I tried to use your father-in-law to get at you. But, you . . . you got too big for yourself. I knew when you came all the way into this business and started making deals you would think you were the boss of everything. I let you have the shine for a little while. Yes, you were living like a boss for a bit, but you got too big," the tall, ugly, man with red rat eyes hissed as he came into focus. He had stepped around the bright light, and Antonio could now see every feature of his face.

"Just let them go. I'll do everything you ask, King. I was always loyal to my father. He gave me a job. I just did my job. I came into this business because I wanted to save my family. I did everything he asked of me, but I didn't know anything about your deals with Emil. My wife and son had nothing to do with it. I gave up everything, even my wife. This business took the only woman that I ever truly loved from me. What more can I do? Now you're about to take my family, I'll give it all up. Just tell me what you want," Antonio cried as another round of punches landed in his midsection. More cracks and coughs came as the men pounded on him, breaking bones and injuring his insides

Paige winced and turned her face away. Her heart was breaking, watching him suffer. It was worse than any pain she could ever go through with his lying and cheating.

"Daddy! Stop hurting my Daddy!" Christian screamed. Paige quickly slapped her hand over his mouth. It was killing Paige to know he was in all of that pain. After she discovered what Antonio had done, yes, she was devastated, but that didn't change the fact that she loved him and that he was all she and her son had in the world.

"Just let them go," Antonio rasped. It was his last-ditch effort to save them all. He recognized that the position they were in right at that moment was all his fault. Paige had once pleaded with him to leave the business and the Cartwright's alone. She had asked him to stop being in the streets and to just get a regular job. Paige knew how stubborn he could be, and there was nothing much she could do about it. He was determined to show her he could provide for them. Antonio was the type of dude that never backed down from something that he wanted. As much as Paige hated it, she also admired it in a lot of ways. Now, they were all facing death with no clear way out of the situation. All because of Cartwrights. If anyone deserved to die, it was Emil.

"Paige, I'm so sorry! I just wanted the best for us. I just wanted to make things better. I never meant to have this happen to you. I told you, King! Just kill me and let my family go! It is me that you want! I was the one who worked with Emil and pulled the lid off of your business! It was all me . . . not them!" Antonio cried some more.

"Shut the fuck up! I'm tired of your fucking mouth. You and your brother here, and the rest of you bastards cost me millions of dollars because you motherfuckers wanted to stage a fucking takeover . . . now I want to see all of you bastards suffer. You're a piece of shit, just like your father. You're not worth sharing the same air with," King barked, waving his hands.

His goons immediately surrounded Antonio. His heart rattled in his chest, but there was nothing else they could do to him that would hurt him more than the possibility of Paige and Christian dying at his hands. Antonio gave up at that moment. Whatever was going to happen must've been fate from the beginning, he reasoned with himself.

After a few minutes, one of the huge thugs dragged Antonio across the gravel floor. It was like nothing he had ever felt before. He didn't know how after all of those hours of torture, he hadn't slipped into shock. His entire body felt like someone had doused him with gasoline and lit him on fire. He could feel the skin on his legs shedding away against the rough floor. He didn't want to die, but if he was going to die, he was going to go out fighting. He tucked his bottom lip under his top teeth and snarled.

"Get off of me! Get the fuck off of me!" Antonio growled so loudly his throat itched. "Fuck all of you! You're all going to burn in hell for what you're doing!" he continued, feeling blood rushing to places on his body that he didn't remember even existed. Antonio bucked his body wildly, but all of his fighting efforts were to no avail. Of course they were stronger than him. Of course he wasn't going to be able to break free, but it just made him feel slightly better inside that Paige and his son could at least see him try.

Antonio had never dreamed of going out of this life on his knees. The man dragging him finally roughly let go of and released him with so much force that his head slammed to the floor. Antonio felt something at the base of his skull come loose. He was dazed for a few seconds, but not for long. He was brought back to reality when he felt a boot slam into his ribs. The force was so great that a mouthful of blood spurted from his mouth.

"You don't have all of that back up now," the goon hissed.

"Please don't hurt him anymore. I will get my father to give you everything we have if you just let him go," Paige cried out.

There was evil laughter. "It is too late for that. Your husband, or whatever he is to you now, should've thought about that before he and his family betrayed me. Now, someone has to pay with their life. There will be no more talking," the man said with finality. The next thing Paige heard was the ear-shattering explosion of a gun.

"No," she belted out, and she shut her eyes. But when she opened them, Antonio was still there, panting, and one of Max King's henchman was lying dead next to him. Everyone was whipping their heads around to find the source of the shot, when Paige heard a voice entirely too familiar to her.

"King," boomed the voice of Gladstone Tillary through the room, and from behind a stack of boxes emerged Senator Tillary and three of what Paige recognized as high-ranked political consultants, who King and the Cartwrights knew as his muscle. But the gun was in Gladstone's hand. Another shot rang out, and the man who had stood above Paige fell to the ground next to her, the blood leaking from his chest pooling around him and spreading out in a circle that touched her shoes. Another shot rang out, and the last of King's crew hit the ground.

King looked at his dead protection and didn't even shudder, he just stood up straight and kicked the body out of his way. "Hello, Gladstone," he said with a smirk malicious enough to set his own face on fire.

Paige was wondering why her father hadn't looked her way yet. Her mind was not in the place to process the implications of how her father had found them so quickly, or of how he had killed a man, she was only grateful to see him.

"King," her father boomed again, walking further and further toward the center of the room where King kneeled over the bloodied Antonio. "I do not care about your business, in fact, all I have ever done is protect it, is to scratch your back while you scratch mine." Gladstone was flying across the floor, it was almost as though he was possessed, Paige suddenly lost her father to this crazed man. He put his gun up again and suddenly he was standing right in front of King, Antonio on the floor, gasping under him trying to recover his breath.

"Welcome," smiled King, looking like the devil incarnate, "I'm glad you could finally make it." The two men stood eye to eye. Of all the years they had spent together, constantly on the edge of destruction, the one thing that had kept them accountable was that they both had everything to lose. King knew it, and Gladstone knew it, that this was the final battle. There would be no moving past this.

"My daughter," growled Gladstone. His henchmen moved in behind him, and King was outnumbered. "My daughter," he screamed, louder, his voice taking up every bit of air in the room. "My daughter, you do not touch. There is not much that we hold sacred, but you know better than this," whispered Gladstone, but everyone could hear him from the pain and the bass his voice held.

"I know," said King quietly, his smile slowly fading into anger, "but it is not my fault that this is the company your daughter has chosen to keep." Antonio was still at his feet. He kicked him like a dog that has misbehaved, and Antonio barked out like one.

Even in his painful delirium, Antonio hated that his father-in-law was there. He finally knew for certain that he would have rather died than to have lost his dignity the way that he had. But it was too late now, there Gladstone stood above him, being the man in the situation. He hated it. Antonio fought against his own body to get up, to try and do something, to help. The body that for so long had been the key to his success, the body that had got him out the hood, that had got him his nice life and his beautiful woman, that body he was so proud of, was betraying him when he needed it the most. Antonio raised himself up onto his hands and then fell again, his body hitting the ground hard. King and Gladstone were so deep in their hate of each other that they didn't notice him moving around at their feet.

"My daughter is not her husband," said Gladstone, "she is not the Cartwrights, she is not in this business, in this world."

"She became a part of this world the minute her stupid-ass fuck of a husband tried to get into his daddy's business," spit King back at him. They glared at each other.

"No," Senator Tillary responded, "she is innocent. I don't care what you say. You cannot do this to my daughter, to my grandson, and think that you can get away with it. Max, this is the last straw, I promise you this is the last straw." He cocked his gun.

King began to laugh. He put his hands on his knees and threw back his head and he roared with laughter. Everything was quiet except for Christian's cries and King's gasps of hysterics. Gladstone kept his gun cocked and on him, but King just kept laughing.

"Motherfucker," yelled King, "you think you can kill me? You honestly think you can kill me?"

Below the two men, Antonio was still struggling to move. There were so many bodies around him, dead and otherwise, he didn't know where to put himself, but he was slowly, slowly crawling his way toward Paige and his son, to the only two things that mattered.

"We've been playing at this game for a long time, King. We have. And honestly, I have enjoyed our time together, but it's time it comes to an end." His gun was between King's malicious, bloodshot eyes. King pushed his forehead against the barrel of the gun. Gladstone stood his ground, and the skin on King's forehead moved in ripples against the pressure of Gladstone's rage.

"Do it, motherfucker, do it," King said, "I dare you."

Gladstone considered the threat. He had just killed a man about five minutes before this moment. For all intents and purposes, he should have no hesitation, as murder was not something that was foreign to him. But he couldn't pull the trigger. Antonio, who had managed to make his way out from beneath them, could feel the hesitation radiating off of his father-in-law, and from where he lay on the ground could see where Gladstone was looking, which was directly into King's eyes, and not on his hands which were slowly making their way toward the gun on his hip. Antonio could feel that bad thing, that scary thing that had been living in him that he had been pushing down, rise up and take over his broken body. Gladstone pushed the gun harder into King's forehead and King kept laughing and laughing, the whole time his hand moving. The bad thing in Antonio took over.

"Stop laughing," Gladstone bellowed, and King pulled his gun in the loudness of his opponent's yelling.

Paige, who had been watching the whole time, screamed and covered Christian's eyes, sure that her father was about to die, taking the only chance of her and her son's salvation with him. The crack of the gun rang out and she closed her eyes, screaming and screaming. From behind her eyelids, she could hear the thud of a body hit the floor. Her body shook with sobs and she shook Christian's small body with her own as he buried his face in her chest. King may die at the hands of Gladstone's men, but she could not imagine life without her father. She could hear low talking and wondered why there hadn't been the second gunshot, the one that was needed to kill King. As much as it scared her, she opened her eyes. In front of her was a scene she could not believe.

On the ground, bleeding from the shot to his head, was Max King. Laying on the ground, panting with exertion, was Antonio, gun still in his hand. Her father was looking down at his long-time partner and was speaking quietly to one of his men. Paige grabbed Christian in her arms and had to make the decision between whether she would go to her father or to Antonio, but seeing him bloodied and beat the way he was, the wall around her heart broke down and she chose Antonio, almost instinctively, putting Christian down on the ground next to him. His eyes were still alert, even though the skin around them was swollen. He looked at his wife and his son, in disbelief that they had somehow made it out alive.

Gladstone stopped talking to his goon and looked at what was happening between his daughter and her disgraced husband. He hated that Antonio had been the one to kill King, but as things stood he was at the very least glad that someone had done it. He looked down at the blood that was pooling around his shoes and stepped back to ensure that his Gucci loafers wouldn't be ruined by something so base as blood.

"Antonio," Paige started, "you saved us."

When Jackson and Emil walked into the hospital room to see Hayden and Antonio side by side in their own beds and Senator Gladstone Tillary in between them, they almost turned around and left. Emil and the Senator had interacted before, and it was never pleasant considering Gladstone spent all of his time trying to put Emil behind bars on behalf of Max King. But King was dead now, thanks to the Cartwright bloodline, and that was something that Emil could hang onto in the battle of pride that was about to go down.

"Emil," said Gladstone seriously.

"Senator Tillary," said Emil, his words dripping with false politeness like it had been coated in oil before it came out of his mouth. "This is my son, Jackson, and it appears as though you have already met my other son," he said, gesturing to the unconscious Hayden in his hospital bed. Gladstone chuckled.

"And of course, the third son," he said, pointing to the awake Antonio, who was glaring at Emil. He blamed him for this, even though he really should have been blaming himself for having gotten into the business in the first place.

"Senator," said Emil, "you should have known better than to have gotten involved in street affairs." He was not the kind of man to beat around the bush, and he had come to the hospital for one thing and one thing only: to fix the mess that killing Max King had caused. "Politically, you know this is a disaster. I know that you will find someone to pay off to keep your name out of the news, but as for my sons, this will ruin them if Paige has to testify about what went down in that warehouse and everything before it. Help me, help you, protect your daughter."

It was at that moment that Paige walked in holding two coffees, one for her, and one for her father who she had been so grateful had stayed by her side the whole time. Everyone in the room turned to look at her. She gulped.

Chapter 13

The End or The Beginning?

Paige curled the fingers of her left hand into her palm in an attempt to stop the trembling. She squeezed so tight her knuckles paled, and her perfectly French-manicured nails (the only thing that seemed the same in her life) left half-moon shaped dents behind. Her heart punched against her chest wall and fine droplets of sweat cropped up at her hairline.

"You have to do this, Paige. Remember that," she mumbled to herself. She'd thought all sorts of things within the past ten seconds. Would she bother going through the process of changing her name to Paige Roberts again after she'd already changed it back to Paige Tillary? Would she go on a honeymoon this time since she'd suffered morning sickness and stayed in bed the entire seven days the first time? She shook off those silly thoughts. Of course not! A marriage of convenience didn't call for all of those things. Right?

Her brain started with the questions again. Paige swallowed hard so that her sparkly diamond choker rose and fell against the ladder of her throat. She would've paced in circles if she didn't have on what she called her thirty-minute heels—the kind you wear for making rounds at an event and slip off after thirty minutes.

"We are almost ready for you," Donna, the venue host said, interrupting Paige's thoughts.

Paige turned around, smiling beatifically. She'd been practicing that smile all morning.

Donna patted her shoulder. "You look amazing, by the way. I can't believe how fast you pulled this together. Amazing."

Paige nodded and shifted her weight from one foot to the other, balancing carefully on her custom made, Swarovski-crystal-covered Manolo Blahnik pumps. Despite everything, in true Paige Tillary (or soon-to-be Paige Roberts) fashion, she'd once again gone all out for the occasion. It wouldn't have been authentic if she hadn't. Her family had called her crazy for doing this again.

"So much has happened, Paige. I don't see how you can even consider doing this, again." Her mother had said. *"These people could kill you for God's sake."*

"Don't think that you have to do this. I can help you. I know people . . . powerful people. Just don't do this again, Paige," her father had said.

"Are you ready?"

Paige looked up, startled. She blinked a few times and looked to her right and smiled. "I guess so," she replied, jamming her right fist into her hip, with her arm bent at the elbow to make an opening for her brother to slide his arm through.

"You look amazing, sis."

Paige's stomach clenched. Her father had said almost those exact words the first time she'd gotten married. *You look amazing, baby girl.*

A small explosion of heat lit in Paige's chest—one part anger, one part sadness—as she thought about her father's nerve when he refused to give her away a second time. She closed her eyes and exhaled. She shook her head, wishing away her worries. She couldn't focus on the past right now. If she did, she might not make it down the aisle this time. And this time, the marriage was a necessity, not just a want.

"You clean up nicely yourself." Paige looked up at her brother, her fake smile perfected now.

It was true. Gladstone Tillary, Jr., had come a long way since his latest stint in rehab. Even with his neck tattoos peeking from his shirt collar, he presented well—classy and sharp. Paige was sorry she'd ever gotten him involved in everything that had happened. Her heart broke every time she thought about how she had turned her back on him in his darkest hour, yet he had stood by her in hers.

"I really appreciate you getting rid of those awful dreadlocks, too," she said, her tone playful.

"Well, they're gone but not forgotten," her brother joked, running his hand over his neatly trimmed hair.

They laughed.

Paige needed the laugh. She'd take anything to ease some of the muscle-twisting tension that had her entire body in knots.

Finally, the low hum of her wedding song, *You* by Kenny Latimore, filtered through the outdoor speakers.

"That's our cue."

Her brother squared his shoulders and tightened his lock on Paige's arm, forcing her closer to him.

"Thank you for being here, Junior," Paige whispered. She meant it. She knew he'd probably endured a harsh berating from their parents for agreeing to give her away.

That was the one quality she had always admired most about her baby brother since they were kids. He never cared what her parents said or thought, unlike Paige, who had spent her entire life walking the fine line of being an individual and making her parents happy. She always wanted to be the "good one," as her mother called her.

"C'mon. You know I wouldn't miss the free food and wine," her brother joked.

Paige giggled. Then she got serious. "No wine for you," she chastised in a playfully gruff voice.

"All right. Here we go."

Paige looked down and smoothed her left hand over the fine, hand-sewn iridescent beads on the front of her haute couture gown. She found a lone bead to pick at with the hopes it would help calm her nerves.

"Loosen up. You're a pro at this, right? Second time's the charm?"

Paige parted a quivery-lipped smile. "The way I'm shaking you'd think this was my first time."

She sucked in her breath as she finally stood at the end of the beautifully decorated aisle in the pastoral Breaux Vineyard. One-hundred-year-old weeping willows swayed in the wake of the breeze with their wispy, white bud covered tendrils calling her forward. Pink rose petals dotted the path in the center aisle, and tall silver stanchions holding white and lilac hydrangea globes flanked every other row of white Chiavari chairs. Dreamy, romantic, and heavenly were all words that came to mind.

With her arm hooked through her brother's, Paige plastered on her famous, toothy smile and carefully navigated the vineyard's emerald green lawn in her heels. Collective awestruck gasps rose and fell amongst the guests seated on either side of the decorated bridal path. The absence of her parents and her best friend, Michaela, didn't go unnoticed. But, it was the Cartwrights—Emil, Hayden, and Jackson—who caused Paige to stumble a bit.

Focus, Paige. Focus. She knew they were there to make sure she went through with it, their presence like a threat whispered in her ear. *It'll all be over soon,* she told herself.

Antonio stepped into the aisle to meet her. He wore a smile that said, "I'm trying to make this seem real too." Unlike Paige's penchant for the grandiose, Antonio was simple. He wore a plain black suit, forgoing the obligatory tuxedo, white cummerbund, and shiny shoes.

Paige felt something flutter inside her like a million butterflies trapped in a jar. With everything they'd been through, Paige had lost sight of how handsome Antonio was. He looked more gorgeous now than he had years ago when they were just two young, high school lovebirds. Back then, Antonio was a gangly six-foot-three-inch kid with a bulging Adam's apple and a hairless baby face. Now, he'd transformed into a distinguished gentleman with a neatly trimmed goatee, thick square shoulders that filled out his suit jacket, and a muscular barrel chest. He looked more like a Calvin Klein underwear model than a former professional basketball player. Paige had certainly forgotten. Anger, hurt, bitterness, and the threat of a life sentence had a way of changing perspective, she'd learned.

Antonio took her brother's place at Paige's side. She looked over at him, her heart dancing in her chest.

"Shall we begin with a prayer?" the officiant said, his Bible splayed over his palms.

Paige lowered her eyes. She blinked a few times, remembering where she was and why exactly she was there. This was all part of the agreement that had saved their lives. The wedding ceremony was a blur. It was not until cheers erupted from the small crowd of sixty guests that Paige realized it was done. She'd married Antonio for a second time. To hell with the reasons they had divorced in the first place. The reasons. Thinking about the reasons made Paige think of Michaela, her absence at the wedding as noticeable as a huge sinkhole in the middle of widely traveled road.

Paige felt sick, but still, she flashed a smile.

"And now I can kiss my bride," Antonio beamed, playing his role. Paige welcomed his tongue into her mouth for a long, passionate seal of their vows. It didn't matter what she felt. She knew it would make for better headlines in the media. Better ratings, too. It would also set her in-laws at ease. Remarrying Antonio needed to solve their problems. It needed to save their lives. It needed to right all of the wrongs. It needed to keep her from having to testify against him . . . them.

Antonio and Paige pulled apart and turned toward their spectators. Cheers arose. Paige's cheeks flushed, and the bones in her face ached from grinning. She deserved an Academy Award.

Antonio wore a cool grin as they slowly made their way down the aisle. He squeezed Paige's hand as if to say, "at least this part is over."

"Wait right there . . . hold that pose!" the photographer called out. "Kiss her," he instructed, hoisting his camera to eye level to ensure he captured the exact moment their lips met. The flash exploded around them. Cameras rolled. Money shot after money shot were captured. This was great.

Paige and Antonio turned to each other on cue, their tongues engaged in another scandalously intimate dance. The photographer's flash lit up in front of them like heavenly beams of light, and the crowd erupted in another round of cheers. Perfection.

The sun basked the couple in abundant light and warmth. It was truly the perfect May afternoon for an outdoor wedding. If only everything else in their lives were this perfect.

"Walk slowly forward now," the photographer instructed, the camera crew backing up for the wide angled shots.

When Paige and Antonio finally made it to the end of the aisle, they were bombarded by guests eager to snap photos with cell phones and personal cameras. Noticing the paparazzi disguised as regular guests, Antonio waved like a politician and Paige flashed her debutante smile. Everyone wanted to get the story first.

"Antonio." Jackson Cartwright stepped into their path, clapping his hand on Antonio's shoulder.

Paige's smile faded, and she bit down into her jaw.

"I didn't think you'd go through with it. I'm proud of you. Maybe you're braver than I thought," Jackson said, smiling. He turned his attention to Paige. "Congratulations."

Paige shivered.

"One more!" the photographer shouted, jutting his camera forward for a close-up.

Paige twisted away, happy for the distraction. Antonio and Paige faced each other, their fake happiness hanging over them like a freshly blown bubble. He kissed her chastely on the nose. She giggled at his playfulness. What a performance! Paige pictured them standing hand-in-hand on a stage, accepting a Tony Award for best actor and actress.

"Antonio!" a voice boomed.

Paige's head whipped left, then right. It was hard to determine what direction the voice had come from until it sounded again. This time, louder. More sinister.

Antonio's head jerked to the left. Paige craned her neck, but there were so many people in front of them.

"Antonio!" the voice boomed again. "You should've played by the rules!" Screams erupted as the wedding goers saw the source of the voice first.

"Oh my God! Gun! He's got a gun!" a guest screamed.

Antonio's eyes widened. Frantically, he unhooked his arm from Paige's and stepped in front of her. Before he could make another move, the sound of rapid-fire explosions cut through the air.

Antonio's fake groomsmen, who were really Emil's goons, ran at full speed down the aisle, guns drawn. Dirt and grass flew in their wake as more shots rattled off. Two of the security guards were picked off, falling to the grass like bowling pins. Screams pierced the air from every direction.

Antonio's body jerked from the impact of the bullets. His arms flew up, bent at the elbow and flailing like he was a puppet on a string. His body crumpled like rag doll and fell into an awkward heap on the ground.

Paige stood frozen, her feet seemingly rooted into the earth around her. This was just a bad dream. Another bad dream. Another fucking nightmare. It wasn't real. She couldn't get enough air into her lungs to breathe.

"Antonio!" Paige shrieked, finally finding her voice.

"Get that motherfucker!" someone yelled.

The sounds of tires screeching and more loud booms exploded around Paige. She coughed as the grainy, metallic grit of gunpowder settled at the back of her throat. She inched in the dirt to where Antonio lay, gasping for breath. The smell of bloody, raw meat wafted up her nose. The earth around Antonio pooled into a bright red lake of his blood.

"Antonio!" Paige screamed. Her throat burned with acid. She grabbed his shoulders and shook them, hoping for a response. He had to live, or this would've been all for nothing. Deals had been cut. They had to be remarried to make sure that her father stayed loyal to Max King and to make sure the Cartwrights kept their end of the bargain. Everyone's lives depended on this.

"There's another one!!" a man screamed. "Get him!"

Paige looked up just in time to see the end of a silver gun.

"No!" she sobbed, throwing her body on top of Antonio's. More deafening booms blasted through the air.

Paige hovered between consciousness and oblivion. The thundering footfalls of fleeing guests left her feeling abandoned and adrift. She lay on top of Antonio, her breathing labored. An explosion of heat passed through her body, spreading like wildfire in a California forest. The origin was hard to pinpoint, as the pain seemed to radiate from every pore of her body. *I'm shot.* Her eyes rolled back; then darkness came down on her like a guillotine. Paige had no choice but to welcome the darkness with open arms.

It seemed like eternity when Paige's eyes finally fluttered open. The raging fire in her throat and pounding between her ears indicated that she was *not* dead. No, she was very much alive, and each ache in her body made her painfully aware of that fact. Paige immediately started gagging. She kicked her right foot and lifted her left hand to grab the thick breathing tube running down her throat that was making her gag. The heart monitor next to her bed sounded off with a high-pitched scream. Two nurses rushed toward Paige's bedside. Lillian jumped up from where she had been holding vigil at Paige's side.

"What's happening?" Lillian huffed, panicked and moving toward Paige within seconds.

The nurses ushered Lillian to the side of the room, away from the patient.

"Don't touch me! Do you know who I am? I want to know what's happening with my daughter!" Lillian demanded, ready to fight.

"Please, stay back. We need to treat the patient!" a nurse chastised from Paige's bedside.

Lillian curled her hands into fists. "Bitch, don't push me again!"

Gladstone grabbed Lillian around her waist.

"No! That's my child laying there! They can't just turn me away like that! I want to know what's happening to her!"

The nurse drew one side of the curtain around Paige's bed, shutting her parents out.

"Mrs. Tillary . . . it's going to be okay. Shhh. . . . Don't do that now, you'll injure yourself," a tall nurse with piercing blue eyes said.

"We're going to have to ask you both to step out," the other nurse instructed as she peeked out from behind the curtain.

"I'm not going anywhere!" Lillian boomed. Gladsone tightened his grasp and tugged her toward the doorway.

"I know, I know. Breathing tubes are a bitch when you're awake, but that collapsed lung you got there is worse, so try to relax and let the machine help you. I'll give you something to help you sleep," the short nurse comforted, maternally patting Paige's arm.

Paige's eyes darted up to the television hanging on the wall in front of her bed. The television volume was muted, but close captioning was turned on. Antonio's face flashed on the screen.

FORMER NBA PLAYER, TURNED CRIMINAL, SHOT ON HIS WEDDING DAY.

Irritated, Paige moaned, gagging against the tube again. The heart monitors reacted with a high-pitched screech.

"What's going on?" the nurse returned, hands on her hips.

"Something upset her," the other nurse stated, following Paige's line of vision.

Paige's eyes were glued to the television screen. Warm tears flowed from her eyes, trailing into her hairline. She strained against the arm restraints. Her entire body tensed. Heated daggers of pain shot through her back and shoulder with every movement.

"I think she wants to hear this," the nurse said, nodding toward the television. She grabbed the remote and raised the volume. Paige relaxed her head on the pillow as she listened to the tail end of the newscast.

"Police authorities say when the smoke cleared, four people were found dead, including two alleged gunmen. Six others were seriously injured. So far, police have not offered any speculation about a motive for the tragic wedding day massacre. Police say that Antonio Roberts was working for reputed crime boss, Emil Cartwright.

There is not proof that his ties to Cartwright is directly linked to the shooting."

Scenes from the wedding flashed across the screen before the newscast went to commercial. Paige shifted restlessly in her bed.

"Shhh. . . . You have to stay calm," the nurse comforted as she plunged a sedative into Paige's intravenous line. "This will help," she whispered as the medicine entered her bloodstream. Paige squeezed her eyes shut, and Antonio showed up on the insides of her eyelids. She didn't know if he was dead or alive, or how the rest of their lives would turn out now. She felt more afraid than ever.